"I don't want to marry you, Fiona."

His laugh was mockingly unpleasant. "But that doesn't mean I don't want you. You've become very beautiful in these intervening years. Do you understand me?"

Fiona's heart was pounding within her. Whatever was he driving at? Without waiting for her reply, he crushed her mouth with his.

"Then the engagement is on again," Fiona managed to whisper afterward.

Alan turned away from her. "I thought I'd made that clear. I find you very desirable and am quite willing to have you as my mistress."

Fiona went chalk-white. "Oh, God," she moaned as she made blindly for the door.

His voice came light and firm behind her. "Before you slam that door, one more thing. If you want to change your mind, I'll be right here."

OTHER

Harlequin Romances

by ELIZABETH DAWSON

1878–ISLE OF DREAMS

The Bending Reed

by

ELIZABETH DAWSON

Harlequin Books

TORONTO • LONDON • NEW YORK • AMSTERDAM
SYDNEY • HAMBURG • PARIS • STOCKHOLM

Original hardcover edition published in 1979
by Mills & Boon Limited

ISBN 0-373-02306-5

Harlequin edition published January 1980

Printed in U.S.A.

CHAPTER ONE

'DAD, I can't. I just *can't!*' Fiona wept. She leaned against her father's shaggy cardigan, trying to draw some of his strength into her own body. 'I've thought and thought about it and I know what I *ought* to do. If I have to tell him myself, I . . .' She broke off, twisting herself to look up into those troubled dark eyes above her. 'Oh, Dad, I must go away! Today. Soon. Before he comes to find me. I hate having to ask you to do my dirty work, but I just cannot talk to Alan,' she bit her lip, 'let alone see him.'

Edward tucked his big hand through his daughter's arm and led her to the elderly settee which stood comfortably before the fire. He made her sit down and eased himself beside her.

'I wish you'd tell me what's really wrong between you and Alan. Are you sure this isn't a simple case of pre-wedding nerves? They'll pass as soon as it's over. If you could manage to live through these next three days . . .'

Fiona's shake of the head was vigorous. She blew her nose loudly.

'Dad, I've also thought of so-called nerves, but it isn't that. It's something far, far deeper. I know I can't go through with it. I'm not marrying Alan on Saturday. It would be a terrible mistake. Don't you see, it's better to know *now* than wait until afterwards?'

She could see her father vainly trying to hide his distress. Fiona was not herself, and he was hopeful that the arrival of her fiancé might help resolve the problem.

'You owe it to Alan to tell him yourself.'

'Yes, Dad, I know. But I can't, I just can't! I'm a coward. I want to run away and hide. Oh, I know what I'm doing to you, and how terribly ungrateful I am after everything you've done for us both. Dad, I don't *love* Alan!' Her blue eyes haunted him with their despair. He pulled her hard against him. At this moment she resembled a wild animal caught in a terrible trap. He vowed to do everything within his power to relieve her misery.

'Then you mustn't marry him without love. I'll see him when he arrives on leave. And I'll get my secretary to deal with the cancellation of all Saturday's arrangements.' He sighed wearily as she smiled wanly back at him. 'Where will you go, child? Alan will want to know how to find you. Even if you don't want to speak to him, I fear I shall have the utmost difficulty in preventing him from wanting to see you.'

'I'm going to my friend's country cottage until Alan is due to rejoin his ship. He doesn't know of its existence—and please, please don't tell him how to find me!' Fiona begged, her fingers digging into her father's palms.

'Oh dear!' he shook his head again. 'I can't say I like any of this, but you're my only daughter and it's your happiness which matters to me. However, I think you're underestimating your Alan ...'

'He isn't "my" Alan any longer!' Fiona pointed out in a fierce tone.

'Your Alan,' her father continued, unruffled. 'He's a very forceful man who, I'm certain, loves you dearly. I thought it was such a good match between you both. What's wrong? Is it his age?' Fiona shook her head. 'He's only ten years older, but of course, you're still young at nineteen. Perhaps you two shouldn't have rushed into this engagement. I must admit to you now that I had a few doubts when you first became engaged a year ago. But he has been away a great deal of that time.'

'I know. And that's why I've realised the truth. I . . . I think I must have fallen in love with him too swiftly, because I knew we had only two or three weeks together. Then he sailed and we wrote to each other. And, Dad, I don't *know* him! He's become a stranger to me. It was all a stupid mistake, one I should never have allowed to continue until it was almost too late.'

'Poor Alan! Have you spared him any thoughts at all? Has it crossed your mind that he's looking forward eagerly to seeing you again, and to marrying you on Saturday? When the ship docks early tomorrow morning, he'll be looking for you.'

'I won't be there.' She lowered her gaze. 'I know I'm a selfish pig, thinking only of myself and not of poor Alan, but I can't help it, Dad, because the break must be quick and clean. I'm not meeting him. I'm not even going to be around during the whole of his leave. I shall despise myself later, no doubt, but I don't see any other alternative. *I have to get out of this terrible mess!*'

Her father uttered a short, bitter laugh and rumpled her short brown curls.

'My child, you haven't grown up yet, that's your trouble. I shall tell Alan this, and maybe . . . later, of course . . . he'll realise what I've saved him from. Still, it's a pity, and I'm desperately sorry about it, because I like Alan. I think he'd be good for you, make a woman out of you. Couldn't you reconsider very carefully, bearing in mind all I've said, and talk to him? If you're afraid to see him alone, then I'll sit in on the conversation. Adjudicate, shall we say? Would that make it easier for you, dear?'

'No, Daddy darling, I really can't. Please don't ask too much of me! Call me all the names you like; I know I'm despicable and I loathe myself even at this stage, but I don't see any other way. Alan's going to be hurt badly, and I wish he wasn't. As I told you earlier, my letter ought to be there waiting for him when the ship docks. I expect he'll be given it before disembarkation, because it always takes time to unload the cargo. He'll telephone here afterwards, but I won't be at home. I shall be alone at Julie's cottage, and there's no phone, so I'm relying on you not to give him my address. Promise me, Dad, promise me!'

He regarded her without speaking, his expression grave and troubled.

'Very well,' he said after a long pause. 'Much as it goes against the grain to say this, I'll do exactly as you've asked.' She gave him a wan smile. 'But I'm warning you, child, don't come crying to me in a few weeks' time because you've discovered that after all you've made a terrible mistake and wish you'd married Alan as planned!'

'I won't, Daddy. My mind is perfectly clear. I never want to see Alan Howard again.'

The fortnight Fiona spent at Julie's tiny cottage in the heart of the country passed without incident, although every time she heard a car approach along the narrow lane, her heart would stop and she became very still. Waiting ... waiting ... waiting lest the vehicle brake outside the cottage. Each time the driver continued straight on.

There had been a letter from her father after the second day, a letter which had made her cry very bitterly.

'I've seen and spoken to Alan. Although he tried not

to show it, I know he was deeply hurt by your strange behaviour. However, he and I parted on the best of terms. He asked me to tell you that he wouldn't want you to do anything which is repugnant to you and is thankful you were able to make your decision before it was too late to undo the damage.

Our conversation was short and to the point, then he left. As he said goodbye, he thanked me for my friendship and said it would always be a disappointment to him that it had had to be brought to an end. Well, my dear, I doubt whether we shall either of us see Alan Howard again! When you decide it's safe to come home then I shall be glad to have you with me again. Surely you must be as lonely as I?

Your loving Daddy.'

Fiona cried for a long time, but for what reason she could not say. Was it the unspoken criticism in her father's letter? The fact that Alan had accepted the inevitable without even trying to fight back? Was that it, that he did not consider her worth the effort? If so, then it came as a painful truth, but one which she deserved. She had hit him hard below the belt, and there was no one to blame but herself for the retaliatory punch.

That night Alan figured vividly in her dreams. They were swimming beside a tranquil sea, he, so bronzed and lithe in blue swim-trunks, his arm about her waist as he lifted her to kiss her. The taste of salt was strong on her lips. Then a huge wave came, tearing them apart, and she was floundering ... floundering ... in choking, bitter waters, while somewhere far, far away, Alan's laugh came to her ... mocking, mocking ... She awoke to the taste of salt tears in her mouth.

On the day before the *Heloise Ballard* was due to sail again, Julie suddenly arrived. Blonde, petite, full of fun, Julie was preceded up the garden path by her terrier who leapt at the closed front door, scrabbling with his feet to be let into a domain that belonged solely to him, and from which an intruder had obviously barred him. When Fiona flung open the door, the tiny dog growled and barked at her, pretending to attack in a series of feint rushes. Laughing, she bent to gather him into her arms. All canine animosity was forgotten and a long pink tongue lavished affectionate kisses on every part of Fiona's anatomy within reach.

'Surprise! Surprise!' Julie chuckled. 'Managed to escape the chains of work a day sooner than expected. I knew you'd be needing a little comfort, so here I am. Let me look at you.' She walked round Fiona, frowning intently. 'Mm! Tussles with the old conscience certainly leave their mark! You're looking drawn and wan. Won't do at all, love. Tell me, everything go all right? Did he come and find you after all? Stupid question to ask, Julie lass, 'cos if he had he'd have swept his erring love off her feet and dragged her by the hair to the altar. Where she belongs.'

Fiona could not help smiling.

'No, Julie, it's over for good. And I'm glad. We were wrong for each other. I'd have made his life a hell. Thanks for letting me stay here to fight it out with myself.'

'Bolt-hole, you mean, love,' Julie reminded her briskly. 'Pity I wasn't here. Had your Alan come seeking you, I'd have filched him from under your nose, or had a darned good try at it! However, I'm here for a purpose. It's all over, you say?'

'Yes.'

'Any regrets?'

'Some. For my appalling treatment of him.'

'Guilty conscience, sweet, that's only natural. Shows you're quite a decent girl at heart. And, my love, fonder of him than you think.' Julie wagged an admonitory finger. 'Boat leaves tomorrow?'

'Yes. And it's a ship, not a boat. Alan kept trying to make me use the correct terminology.'

'The cure is absolute?'

'I sincerely hope so.'

'You need proof, I think. So this is what you and I are going to do. I'm driving you to the docks tomorrow ...'

'*No!*' This as a shriek of panic.

'Hold on, hold on! Not to see him face to face, just onlookers. We'll mingle with the crowd seeing off the passengers. You said they take a few?'

'About thirty, but not every voyage is fully booked.'

'I have a friend who works in one of the shipping offices on the quayside. It's all arranged. We can watch the ship from there. Alan will never know you're there.'

'Oh, Julie, why? *Why?* I don't see the point.'

Julie tucked her arm through her friend's, jerking it as she spoke.

'Look, I don't want you to have regrets in the future. You refused to see Alan when he arrived back after ... how long was it?'

'Eight months.'

'Eight months, then. If your memory's anything like mine, you'll have forgotten whether he has a mole near his left temple, what colour his eyes are, whether he had a kissable cleft in his chin, how long he grows his sideboards ...'

'Burns.'

'What matter? You've got to see him again, Fiona. Just look long and hard at him, then close the chapter once and for all. Well?' Her green eyes twinkled with mischief. 'I promise you, if you funk this, I'll put Jo-Jo at your heels to bully you into the car. Isn't that so, Jo-Jo darling?' she cooed at the little dog, who immediately rolled over on to his back on the rug for her to tickle his tummy. 'There you are, a ferocious creature who'll eat you for dinner if I so much as give the word!'

The two girls reached the dreary quayside office without incident the following morning. Throughout the drive past the dock gates and on to the quay, Fiona had been in a turmoil of worry lest inadvertently they should bump into Alan. And if they did, what then? she kept asking Julie, who refused to take such a pessimistic attitude.

'We won't,' she promised, and they did not.

The young man in the office greeted Julie with obvious affection.

'Inspecting the manifest, eh?' he teased, kissing Julie's proffered cheek.

'Of course. Well, what news?'

'He was aboard until about half an hour ago, when he came hurrying ashore for some reason. But he ought to be back any minute. You were lucky not to walk into him.'

Fiona paled and sat down suddenly.

'I shouldn't have come,' she said in a weak voice. 'This is just ridiculous!'

'Come over here, Fiona, and watch from the window.'

'What's the poor man done to warrant all this spying?' Julie's friend wanted to know.

'Never mind. You haven't breathed a word, have you?' Julie asked in a threatening tone.

'Of course not, silly!' The young man grinned at Fiona. 'Secret heart-throb of yours?' Fiona bit her lip so hard that she felt the warmth of blood. 'From what I understand, he's already bespoken.'

'Shut up!' Julie hissed.

The young man obliged by a shrug of the shoulders before turning his attention to a ledger which stood open on a table near the window. Her hands clasped, Fiona stood on his right, her eyes riveted on the outside scene.

After less than five minutes, a uniformed figure strode quickly towards the gangway. Neither girl could see Alan's face until he paused, turned and looked carefully up and down the quay. For some inexplicable reason, Fiona sensed that he was searching for her, yet how could he know she was here?

He did not, of course. His engagement was over and he was a bitter, wounded man. While there was time, surely there might still be hope that she would change her mind and come running along the quay to beg him to forgive her? But he did not want her. Not now. Not after she had made such a fool of him.

Alan strode up the gangway and vanished aboard the shabby vessel that was to be his only home for the next few months.

'Mm!' Julie murmured approvingly beside Fiona. 'He's nice. I like tall men with athletic figures. Uniform suits him, too. Darkly handsome in a rather swarthy way, but ...' she gave a mock shudder, 'I'm beginning to see why you broke it off, Fiona. A man used to having his own way, and hard, I'd surmise. Was that why you did it?'

'I suppose so,' Fiona responded in a weary tone, hoping the young man with the ledger had become deaf. 'Let's go, may we?' She did not want to discuss Alan with anyone.

Seeing him again had filled her with such an aching torment of guilt that she wanted nothing more than to put as many miles as possible between the quayside and herself.

When that ship was edged away from the quay, the chapter in her life could be closed for good.

CHAPTER TWO

WHEN Fiona returned home, she found that her father's secretary had made a list of all the wedding gifts she had received, and had drafted a rough copy of the short note to go with each. All that was left to do was the final packing and postage, and then it would be over. Fiona blessed the presence of the elderly Miss Horness, who had worked for her father ever since he had had his first success in writing. Each year he produced three books: one novel, under what Fiona referred to as 'Dad's flowery pen-name' and two serious works of non-fiction. Fiona rarely read the latter because they were too much above her head, but they brought in a modest sum which was sufficient to keep them all in reasonable comfort, Miss Horness included. Without Miss Horness, there would be no books, Edward had said on many occasions. He had no idea how to use either a typewriter or a dictaphone, relying instead on the power of the spoken word ... and never mind how many times afterwards the whole gist had to be altered!

As the days passed, Fiona gave up wondering whether Alan might write to her. There had been no word at all since his departure, and she could not help secretly admitting to herself that she felt piqued. Oh well, she decided, obviously he must have loved me as little as I loved him. But it hurt, it hurt badly. What else could she expect, running in panic from the man she was supposed to marry?

By tacit agreement, Alan's name was not mentioned in the household, although there were occasions when it came, unbidden, to the forefront of Fiona's mind. Especially the time when she had been doing some hasty Christmas shopping and had caught sight of a tall figure in navy blue uniform standing a short distance from her, choosing silk scarves. Her pulses had thudded, her palms dampened and a tiny cry had arisen to her throat. She could not quite see the man's face, but surely there was something about the way the dark hair grew at the nape of the neck beneath the cap that was unmistakably Alan? She had stared and stared and, becoming conscious of eyes on his back, the man in the uniform had turned slowly round. Two pairs of eyes had met ... those of Fiona and a total stranger ... The urge to shop had fled like a wraith in the night; pain had grown in her chest and there was an unpleasant tingling of tears behind her eyes. That evening, she had been very quiet and withdrawn, causing her father to study her covertly and wonder what was wrong. However, he said nothing and, by the morning, the distressing mood had flown as if it had never been.

Now three years had passed since the *Heloise Ballard* left dock. The recent eighteen months had not been happy ones for Fiona. During a hard winter, her father had taken sick and died within the week, leaving her stunned and heartbroken. Dear Miss Horness had been a tower of strength to her, but finally they had to come to the parting of the ways. As the good soul gently explained, now there was no work for her to do she must look around for a new employer, but any time Fiona felt in the need of a chat about old times, then she was always welcome to call round at the tiny yet immaculate flat on the far side of town.

Because the house was now far too big for one person alone, Fiona was obliged to sell it and invest the money in other securities, as advised by the will's executors. Fiona worked as a librarian in the public library and Julie's flat was conveniently close; Julie wanted a new flatmate, her other having moved from the town on promotion, so the arrangement suited Fiona nicely. This, however, was not destined to last more than a few months because Julie met Frank. Frank was quiet and unassuming, and rather shy when in the company of other people. He and Julie fell madly in love, realised they could not live without each other, and swiftly married, leaving Fiona with a large flat which she did not want. The prospect of advertising for someone to share with her did not appeal, so she set about finding something very much smaller. This naturally took some time, because she was a hard girl to please. In the end she discovered exactly what she wanted. An elderly couple called Dodridge wanted to let out the top floor of their modest home near the west side of town, and Fiona was just the girl they had hoped to find. Both parties were delighted with the arrangement and, although Mrs Dodridge took the greatest care not to interfere in her tenant's way of life, she was soon calling her 'Fiona dear'. Every Saturday morning Fiona would take her own and Mrs Dodridge's washing down to the launderette, then both would hang it out together on the long washing line in the garden at the rear of the house.

One evening, when Fiona let herself into the house and called out her customary: 'It's only me, Mrs D.!' the drawing room door opened and Mrs Dodridge came bustling out to greet her, her face bright with excitement.

'Oh, Fiona dear, we wondered if you could spare us a few moments before popping upstairs? That's if you're not hungry, or have a meal waiting?'

Fiona smiled.

'Certainly I'll come, Mrs Dodridge.' She entered the

warm drawing room where a bright fire blazed in the open fireplace.

'Come over here, dear. Over here and let me take your coat for you,' white-haired Mr Dodridge insisted, reaching for her. She removed her coat and he laid it carefully over the back of a chair before turning to the small table beside the fireplace where he poured drinks. 'You will have a sherry, won't you?'

'Oh, but . . .' Fiona began, then: 'Of course I will. Thank you very much.'

'Will you ask, or shall I?' Mrs Dodridge turned to her husband, eyebrows quirked.

'You, dear, I think.'

'Is the sherry to your liking?'

'Thank you, yes, it's very nice.'

'Good.' Mrs Dodridge parked her ample form in a chair close to Fiona's and leaned forward, her face eager. 'You know we've told you about our married daughter?' Fiona nodded. 'And how she's going on a cruise in two weeks' time?' Again the nod. 'She's been looking forward to it such a lot, and now something's gone wrong. Oh, it's not the operation she had a few weeks ago. That was splendid. But it's the friend she was supposed to be taking with her. For company, you see.'

Fiona had heard about the married daughter's serious illness in very great detail during recent weeks. It had been a difficult operation, but without complications, and the doctor had advised a sea cruise to help recuperation. Mrs Dodridge's daughter had been widowed almost a year before, but had retained her independence, much to her parents' disappointment. They had hoped she might 're-turn to the fold', as they put it, but the offer had been gently but politely refused. Fiona could understand why and knew she probably might have done the same had she been in the other girl's shoes. After the big operation, bookings had been made for Sandra and a good friend. Now something must have gone wrong.

'Sandra's friend is married to a scientist who's been abroad on a project, apparently. Now it appears he's been given leave, just at the time Sandra had planned to go on this cruise. Naturally her friend wants to cancel the arrangement, which leaves poor Sandra in rather an awkward predicament.'

'I understand. Couldn't she go alone?' Fiona asked.

'She could, but it wouldn't be much fun, would it? And she needs company. Female company.'

Fiona's face brightened. 'Oh, I understand now!' she exclaimed with a smile. 'You're going to join your daughter and wonder if I would keep an eye on your husband during your holiday. But of course I will, Mrs Dodridge. You know I'll help in any way I can.'

This, apparently, was not the response the older woman had expected and neither had her husband, who was shaking his head briskly from side to side.

'No, dear, *I'm* not going with her!' Mrs Dodridge laughed. 'I'm very fond of dear Sandra, and she of me, but we're not the ideal companions for such a trip. Had she been in better health, I might have agreed to go with her, but certainly not on a cruise! I can't stand the sea. Shockingly bad sailor, you see. No. We wondered, knowing that you're soon to have your spring holiday from the library ... you did say it was to be within the next month, didn't you? I hope so. Well, Alfred and I thought you might help us out by stepping into the breach. After all, Sandra can't be very much older than you, and you're both young. I think you'd get on splendidly together. Now don't frown like that, dear!

There's no need to worry about the cost, because it's all been paid for. Sandra arranged all that at the very beginning.'

'Oh, but I couldn't possibly accept ...'

'Neither could you afford to pay full cost,' Mr Dodridge intervened. 'No, lass, you leave things as they are. You'd be earning your fare as far as we're concerned, by just being with our Sandra and helping her to get really well again. There's no need to worry if she gets poorly a little on the ship because they have doctors and nurses for that kind of thing. You see, it's the young companionship which she needs so badly at this moment. Operations make you feel so terribly depressed and I think you'd be exactly right to cheer our daughter. Will you do it for us? I know it may come as rather a shock, and a bit of a sauce to you, because you've been making your own plans for holidays, no doubt. But if you *could* see your way ... it would relieve my wife and me of so much worry ... and this winter's been a hard one for everyone, what with the rain and the wind all the time. A little bit of hot Mediterranean sunshine will swiftly tan your pale cheeks and put a sparkle into your eyes.' He paused, smiling, but very tense. Almost as if he were afraid she might turn down the offer, Fiona thought.

A cruising holiday! At this time of year, and without the worry of payment! It was too good to miss. But she could not accept their generosity. Aloud she said:

'Thank you for asking me. I'd like to go very much. It ... it's a large liner, isn't it?' she ventured rather hesitantly, her mind flashing to Alan.

'Of course, dear. One of the best. Sandra wouldn't have chosen any other,' Mrs Dodridge beamed.

Fiona heaved an inward sigh of relief. It had been possible ... although the chances against it happening were probably astronomical . . . that the ship chosen belonged to the shipping line which employed Alan. He had taken a few passengers, but his ships were certainly not in the luxury liner class! Other practicalities forced themselves to the fore of her mind.

'I shall have to have smallpox and cholera injections, won't I?'

'Not for this cruise, dear.'

'Are you sure?' Fiona was doubtful. She had heard some of her colleagues discussing the requirements before departing on foreign holidays.

'Yes. After her operation, Sandra didn't feel up to having to undergo the various inoculations, so she chose a trip which wouldn't need them. It all saves time for you, doesn't it?' Mrs Dodridge turned to pick up a glossy brochure which had been lying on the small table and handed it to Fiona. 'Sandra asked me to let you have this when we saw her this afternoon. She thought you'd like to know all the details as soon as possible. Here,' she flicked through the pages, 'this is the cruise you'll be taking. Lisbon, Lanzarote, Tenerife, Madeira and Vigo, then home again. It looks terribly exciting, don't you agree? And here,' she flicked over two more pages, 'this is your cabin. Sandra has marked it. She hopes you won't mind sharing with her, but it's a two-bedded cabin, with your own shower and toilet.' She glanced at Fiona's face. 'Do you mind sharing with someone you don't know? It was arranged like that for the company, you understand. Sandra thought it better not to be on her own. In case she needs anything, you see, dear, because she certainly isn't at all strong. But you won't have to do any nursing, or anything like that, because the shipping line already know about her recent visit to hospital and the ship's doctor and nursing staff will be briefed to watch over her. Your job mainly is to keep her cheerful and to help her up on deck, and little things like that. It won't be too irksome for you, will it? Let me reassure you that you won't be tied hand and foot to Sandra, like some kind of nursemaid, because you'll have plenty of time to go off and play deck tennis and swim, or whatever it is people do when they're at sea for days on end. And I expect there'll be plenty of interesting people on board to meet and get to know. It'll help take Sandra out of herself and restore her former good spirits, because she really is very down in the mouth at the moment. I wish she had come here to stay with us after she left hospital, but she refused.' Mrs Dodridge's expression was one of sadness tinged with pride. 'She always was a stubborn girl in some ways, wanting to stand firmly on her own feet after David's death, but we are her parents after all. However, there's the problem of my blood pressure and everything else, so we couldn't persuade her. She wouldn't hear of adding work to the household, as I think I told you some days ago after she had the operation. I tried to tell her it wouldn't be work, but pleasure, but you young things are so horribly independent these days!' she finished on a drawn-out sigh.

'The wife's health isn't of the best, as you must have realised, Fiona,' Mr Dodridge added, just to clarify an already very clear point. 'We miss Sandra, but of course she was quite right.' He slid an arm about his wife's plump shoulders. 'You're as important as she is, and neither of us wanted you to get ill on Sandra's account. Besides, we've seen her every day since she left hospital, and now we have Fiona here to make sure she gets better as quickly as possible.' He smiled rather shakily at Fiona. 'It's grand of you to step into the breach like this, my dear. I don't know what poor Sandra would have done had you refused. Cancelled her cruise, I suppose. Thank you, thank you from the bottom of our hearts.'

Fiona felt a little embarrassed by all this praise and tried to shrug it off.

'No, Mr Dodridge,' she replied, 'it's *you* who must be thanked. This is the most wonderful opportunity ever to come my way, and I shall always be grateful to you both. You can rely on me to take care of your daughter, and to bring her home again fit and well, I promise.'

The time seemed to fly as Fiona prepared for her holiday cruise. It was incredible what had to be done, and how many tiny details there were to attend to before the day she was due to sail. She spent many free hours shopping for last-minute additions to her wardrobe, and even then wondered what vital item she had overlooked. There was a new swimsuit, two new summer dresses, a lightweight cardigan, and some very swift renovations to the evening dress she had purchased four years before and rarely worn. Its style now was rather outdated, but with Mrs Dodridge's advice and some skilful needlework on the part of both of them, they managed to transform it into a chic and beautifully simple garment which looked as if it had been bought from one of the smartest dress salons. When she tried it on for the final fitting, Fiona spun slowly round while the older woman studied the effect with thoughtful and praising eyes.

'Yes,' she remarked with great satisfaction, 'we have it exactly right now. The low sweep of material over your bust here, and the swathes falling delicately below the waist ... oh, it's *perfect*, my dear! That soft apricot shade is so absolutely *you*. You have a lovely figure, too.' Her eyes twinkled mischievously. 'You'll put my poor Sandra in the shade and have all the young officers falling at your feet like ninepins as soon as you set foot on the dance floor. They'll all be madly in love with you before the cruise is two days old!'

'I sincerely hope they won't be!' Fiona responded. 'Most of the officers will be married, with wives of their own left happily at home.' She smiled softly. 'If they weren't married, I expect they'd all be very young, and I don't relish the prospect of putting my life in the hands of a young and green crew. No, thank you! I trust most sincerely that they're old and staid, mature men; age and responsibility go hand in hand.'

Mrs Dodridge was not to be deterred, however. 'I shall stick to what I've said; you'll be having the unattached men falling in love with you; just wait and see!'

Privately, Fiona decided that her landlady was being over-optimistic concerning the tendencies of the opposite sex to fall in love willy-nilly; although she had heard and read of so-called 'shipboard romances' which were wonderful while they lasted, and immediately forgotten after the cruise had ended. Some girls, however, tended to believe in the sincerity of such romance and suffered acutely when disillusionment finally set in. She knew this would never happen to her, because she would not permit herself the folly of losing her heart to a man she might never see once the cruise was over. Since her unhappy affair with Alan Howard, she had not found another man to take his place. In a strange way, she had loved Alan ... until the close proximity of their wedding when she had come to realise her love was not sufficiently deep. She regretted the manner of their parting, regretted it deeply, but how otherwise could she have brought about a clean break? At work, there had been two, if not three young men who had shown considerable interest in her, but nothing had come of the friendships. Not from want of trying on their part, either! she thought ruefully. It was just that ... there was something lacking ... in herself or the young men, she could not determine. No one had taken Alan's place, and she had been perfectly content to leave it that way. No doubt she would remain a spinster for the rest of her life, now and again rueing the day she had sent Alan from her, perhaps. Who could tell? In the meantime, there was the excitement of the cruise to anticipate, and last-minute packing to complete. Was there anything she ought to have put in which had been forgotten? Travel sickness pills? She hoped vehemently that she would not become a victim of any really rough seas that might be encountered, but it was advisable to be prepared, just in case. Possibly there would be remedies to be had on board ship, if so required. And she must remember to put in that list she had made, so that no one would be neglected when she began sending back to England postcards of the stopping-off places. Her friend Caroline had been to Tenerife last year, so she must wait for a postcard from Madeira or Vigo.

There was still such a lot to be done, and they were sailing in less than forty-eight hours!

Mrs Dodridge exclaimed with delight as she stepped into the cabin behind Fiona and Sandra.

'This really is lovely!' She looked around her in appreciation while, behind, her husband also nodded his approval. With four people in the two-bedded cabin, it was rather cramped, so Fiona moved to the porthole, standing slightly on tiptoe to look out at the grey dockside buildings which were almost entirely enveloped in the steady drizzle that was falling.

'Well, dears, much as we'd like to remain here chatting

to you, I really think we ought to be making our way back again. Wouldn't do to sail with you by mistake!' Mrs Dodridge laughed. 'Even though I'm tempted by the comfort of this cabin. Just look at the carpet ... a beautiful shade of mauve. Which reminds me, that old mat near the front door ... don't you think we might replace it with one this shade instead of the beige I was thinking of until now ... ?'

Her husband shrugged, then slid an arm about his daughter's thin shoulders.

'Have a lovely time, darling,' he said. 'And mind you come back fit as a fiddle. Rearing to go, so to speak.'

'I'll see that she does, Mr Dodridge,' Fiona promised as father and daughter kissed each other goodbye. 'It was kind of you to come and see us off.'

'We'll be on the quayside to wave,' Mrs Dodridge reminded both girls. 'Oh, not a moment too soon! There's the bell for all visitors to go ashore. I'll kiss you once again and then we must make haste.' She kissed Sandra and then flung her arms about Fiona, who almost recoiled in surprised delight. 'You're a *good* girl to do this for us all. Mind you enjoy yourself, and come home with a lovely suntan!'

Sandra found it hard to walk fast or climb stairs, but Fiona's hand guiding her assisted them both through the crowd which was flocking on to the deck to wave to those remaining behind. The two girls found a vacant space at the rail and stood together, smiling down at the people on the quay side.

''Bye, Mum! 'Bye, Dad!' Sandra whispered, knowing her parents could not hear as the great liner was edged carefully away from the quay. A tug hooted; another responded, water churned violently in the ever-increasing gap between hull and dockside; even the drizzle lifted temporarily to allow a thin shaft of pale yellow sun which bathed the moving liner in light. As the distance increased, faces on the dockside dwindled into nonentity and finally the crowd itself became one homogeneous blur of drab mackintoshes and coats. The passengers started to move away from the rail and return to their cabins. Sandra reached for Fiona's hand and squeezed it. Her eyes were warm as the two girls studied each other.

'You realise I wouldn't have had the courage to come alone, don't you? I shall always be grateful to you for forgoing your own holiday in order to help me out.'

Fiona laughed with slight embarrassment. 'Believe me,' she replied, 'this kind of holiday is certainly no hardship to me. I'd never have had the chance to plan a cruise for myself. We're going to have fun, aren't we? Shall we go below now, because I think you should rest before dinner. This has been quite arduous for you, what with the journey from home, and all these stairs and things.' She slid her hand through Sandra's arm. 'After a few days, you'll be able to have much more exercise, as long as you take things carefully and gradually. Besides, from all I hear about the Bay of Biscay, it can be quite nasty at times. However, this is a huge liner, so only the very worst of weather would be likely to affect it, especially as it's been fitted with stabilisers. We're due in Lisbon on Tuesday morning, which will give us good time during the first two days to find our sea-legs.'

Dusk was setting in quickly. The cabin appeared gayer than when seen in daylight, with its highly polished furniture and bright bedspreads in a striped pattern of blue and gold. Fiona plumped down on her bed, testing the springs.

'Gorgeous!' she sighed. 'How's yours? While you rest, I'll unpack for you and you can tell me where to put your things. Which of the four drawers would you prefer? I suggest you have the top two, then you won't have to bend down so frequently and strain your scar.'

'Nonsense!' Sandra chided. 'It'll do me good. Besides, by the time the end of the cruise comes I ought to be nearly as good as usual.'

Fiona stood up and began to open suitcases. She turned to the dressing chest and picked up the folded, printed card which lay there. Without more than glancing at the coloured photograph of the liner on its outside, she handed it across to her companion.

'I expect this tells us the gen about who's who and what's what.'

Idly Sandra opened the card and began to read.

'Captain is Alan Howard. First Officer John Hobday. Purser George Thomas. Our steward ... written in pen and ink here, is ...' but Fiona was no longer listening. At the sound of the captain's name she had become very still, her mouth opening in disbelief. But it simply *could not be*! she thought. It must be a quirk of the name. After all, Alan was a fairly common christian name and there certainly was nothing unusual about Howard for a surname. Yet the coincidence was quite incredible.

'... and we're to sit at the doctor's table for meals,' Sandra concluded, and then looked up. 'Why, whatever's wrong?' Her eyes flickered to the nylon nightie in Fiona's hands. 'Is something wrong with that?'

Quickly Fiona pulled herself together, saying:

'N ... no. I just thought I might have forgotten something, and was racking my brains to remember. It can wait.' She turned her back to Sandra and busied herself over the drawer. The other girl continued to talk to her and, somehow, she managed to answer in a coherent manner.

Alan Howard ... Alan Howard ... but why should it be the same man? This luxury liner was a far cry from a battered, superannuated tin tub which had plied its way across oceans for many, many years. Besides, Alan had not worked for this particular shipping line. All the same, her common sense reminded her, three years is a long time, and he had mentioned looking for something a little better. Her banana boat captain! she thought, recalling the occasions when she had teased him about his captaincy. *Had* he been promoted? It was possible, of course, but highly improbable when one considered the great number of suitable candidates for a diminishing number of high-ranking vacancies. No, it could not be the same Alan.

You'll be able to find out for sure when you see the captain yourself, a tiny voice prompted. But when might that be? Tonight? At dinner? Or would the captain be too busy to come to the dining-room?

Thank heaven they had not been put at the captain's table for meals, she decided. That was a privilege reserved for a very few and, thank heaven once more, neither she nor Sandra warranted such distinction. It would be nice, however, to sit at the doctor's table. Perhaps they had been chosen for this because, technically speaking, Sandra was in his charge during the voyage, and it would be a good opportunity for him to keep an unobtrusive eye on her without having to send for her to visit his surgery each morning.

Almost as if she had conjured him up with her thoughts, there came a knock at the cabin door and the doctor announced his arrival.

Fiona opened the door to find a sandy-haired, round-faced young man smiling broadly at her.

'My name's Maynard,' he said. 'I wanted to introduce

myself without delay. I have one of you two ladies on my list.' His eyes flickered past Fiona and came to rest on Sandra who was still sitting on her bed.

'Will you come in, please?' Fiona asked, realising with a jolt that she could not expect the doctor to remain on the threshold for ever.

'Thank you.'

She closed the cabin door behind him and then introduced her companion. He stepped forward, shook Sandra's hand and slid his fingers deftly round her wrist to feel her pulse, smiling all the time. She searched his face with her eyes and began to smile back.

'Nice and steady,' he remarked, after a moment, replacing her hand on her lap. He thrust both hands casually into his trouser pockets as he continued to study her with a distinctly professional air. 'How are you feeling? A little done up, no doubt, after all the hustle and bustle of boarding.'

'I am tired, yes,' Sandra admitted.

'You mustn't overdo things all at once. Take things gradually and, with the sunshine and good weather, you'll start to mend rapidly. I have all the details in my surgery. Your G.P. wrote me an explanatory letter and I'm happy to tell you that there's no special treatment you should have, other than not over-exerting yourself, and resting a great deal. You feel better for the operation?'

'I think so, although I get terribly tired and sometimes feel rather depressed. And the traffic seems to be rushing at me.'

'A natural reaction, all of which will pass.' The doctor turned towards Fiona who was quietly packing away underwear in the top drawer. 'Your friend looks remarkably fit,' he smiled.

'Thank you, yes, I am.'

'Good. If you're worried about anything, please don't hesitate to ring me. But I don't expect complications at all. I spoke to the Chief Steward about tables, and you're eating at mine. I trust that pleases you both?' Fiona nodded, while Sandra said nothing. The doctor grinned. 'I can't have the captain taking the pick of the bunch on every cruise, so I like to get my oar in early! I make the excuse that I ought to have my convalescents firmly under my eye all the time, and it certainly pays dividends now that I've met both of you!' He winked at Fiona. 'Without this ruse I think my captain would saddle me with middle-aged widows and gouty old gentlemen, keeping all the attractive young ladies like you to himself. But don't breathe a word to anyone that I've told you this, otherwise I'll have the wrath of God down upon my head!'

'Why? Is ... is Captain Howard rather a tyrant?' Fiona managed to ask, controlling her feverish curiosity.

'Not in the least. He's a good man, but we all like to keep up our little rivalries. Being the captain, he's entitled to choose whom he wishes to sit at his table. And you usually find that people who are unwell when they take cruises for the purposes of their health are normally well past the prime of life. That's why I get them, to make sure no one takes a turn for the worse while out of my sight. However, I won a point with you two. I told him I must have my patients where I can see them, and he had to give in. I hope you won't be disappointed. You see—well, the skipper's rather attractive and most young ladies are inclined to be foolish where he's concerned. They lose their hearts to him, although it's to no avail, because he's immune to feminine wiles.'

'Married, I suppose?' Fiona suggested.

'No. But very eligible, if only he'd show some interest. For a good-looking man in his thirties he should have been snapped up long ago. But that's life, I suppose. So, Mrs Stern, I must insist that you steer clear of my superior's charms, otherwise your recovery could be severely delayed.' He grinned infectiously. 'Besides, what about me to step into the breach? Do I see you both at dinner tonight?'

'Yes,' Fiona replied, following him to the door and holding it as he passed out into the passage. 'We'll see you then.' She closed the door and returned to Sandra. With a tiny laugh, she asked:

'Well, what did you think of *that*? A bit of a lady-killer himself, I'd say.'

'Oh no! I thought he was utterly charming, and doing his best to put us both at ease. All that waffle about the captain is probably just the line he uses to win our confidence. I can understand his pleasure at finding us to be young.' Sandra wrinkled her nose in laughter. 'He's right, you know. Most people cruising for their health are the over-indulged, obese, heart-attack-prone hypochondriacs well past their prime of life. If he has to suffer them at his table day after day, life certainly must seem tedious. I wonder what the captain is really like? Ugly and cross, I expect. All that twaddle was said just to tease us both. Disillusionment must follow.'

For dinner that night, Fiona chose a soft pink dress with long sleeves and a delicately embroidered neckline, which meant that she had no need of jewellery other than the gold stud ear-rings which had been her favourite for years. She slid her feet into simply-styled brown pumps with slender heels and then brushed her hair until it fell naturally into gentle waves just behind her ears. Sandra was undecided about what to wear, so Fiona selected a rich red dress in courtelle with a brilliant white, almost Peter Pan collar. She helped coil the thick black hair until it was pinned neatly at the nape of Sandra's neck. Standing back to view the effect, she murmured approval.

'Snow White in person. Black hair, like a raven's wing, white skin and red lips.'

'Hardly!' Sandra chuckled. 'Pale white face, yes, but not the white of alabaster. And the red comes from the dress.'

'You must eat well tonight. Are you ready?'

Together they left the cabin and made their way through the narrow passage towards the lift which would take them down to the restaurant deck. They entered the after-restaurant and waited a few moments until a waitress hurried forward to help them.

'We're to sit at the doctor's table,' Fiona said. The girl smiled.

'That will be in the forward restaurant, madam,' she replied. 'If you would care to take the lift back to the main deck and then go forward until you reach the main entrance to take the lift again.'

'Can't we go this way?' Sandra asked, with a frown, thinking of the tedium of walking.

'I'm sorry, madam, but the remainder of this deck is taken up with the kitchens and pantries. However, if you would prefer to dine here, I can see the Chief Steward and make the arrangements.'

Fiona slid her arm beneath her friend's.

'Thank you, but we can manage perfectly well. Just take your time, Sandra, there's no hurry.' Once again she smiled her thanks at the waitress and they turned to leave the restaurant.

'How silly of us!' Sandra scolded. 'It was written down

on that printed card we were given.'

'Never mind. A short walk will sharpen our appetites.'

They made their way to the forward restaurant without further mishap. It was a large, well-lit room, with big windows running down each side so that one could look straight out on to the sea. Now, however, it was dark outside, making everything beyond the windows appear black and velvety. The head waiter came forward and Fiona told him whose table they wanted. With a slight, almost old-fashioned bow of the head, he led them majestically across the thick plush carpet towards one of the round tables set near a window. They were the first to arrive, Fiona noted, as all ten places were unoccupied.

'Are we too early?' Sandra whispered rather apprehensively.

'I hope not,' Fiona replied with a giggle. The waiter smiled and asked where they would care to sit. 'I like watching other people,' Fiona said, and thanked the waiter when he pulled out her chair.

They were not left alone for long. Almost immediately after they were settled, a rather harassed-looking woman in a dowdy dark green dress and with a deep frown hurried across the floor in the wake of the waiter, towing a reluctant small boy after her.

'Mum, I don't *want* any supper tonight!' the child was saying in a penetrating tone.

'You'll do as I say, and sit here until you're told you can get up again,' came the scolding reply.

The boy looked about ten and was stick-thin. Plainly he was very ill at ease amongst so many adults and, after he had been seated, he fidgeted with his feet under the table, occasionally kicking Fiona quite hard. After the third blow she leaned over, smiled, and said quite pleasantly:

'Would you mind, please?'

'Now what are you doing, Tommy?' his mother snapped. 'Really, I don't know why you had to come with us! Taking the measles just when you did, and the doctor saying a sea trip would do you good.' She turned her attention to Sandra, who was eyeing the child with a gentle smile. 'Been a nuisance all the time so far, he has. His aunt and I were going on this cruise, then he goes and gets the measles. Not just gets them, you see, but has complications afterwards. Nothing like sea air, the doctor said. Not just the air at Brighton, oh no! Has to be the warm Mediterranean air, and come with his aunt and me he has to. Now my sister's feeling queasy already and ...'

Whatever she was about to say died on her lips as a deep voice boomed:

'So this is the doctor's table! And where may I sit, pray? Bottlin-Mabee's the name, which you'll all have heard of, of course. Bottlin-Mabee, *the* furniture people.' A vast, bejewelled bosom swept before Fiona's startled gaze and the lady with the imposing name sat down with a bump in her chair. 'Of course, I would have preferred to sit at the *dear* captain's table, as I did this time last year when I came on a cruise, but it was deemed advisable for me to be near the doctor.' A many-ringed left hand tapped the brocaded bust as if it were some kind of treasure. 'It's my heart, you see. Not too good. Far better to have the good doctor near by. Although, of course, as I told *dear* Captain Howard, the doctor really is *far* too young to hold such responsibilities ...' Her dark, rather malevolent eyes fastened on the boy, who was now cringing in his seat. 'And *why* are you still up? Surely supper for children is at an earlier hour?' She wrinkled her nose in acute disapproval and then turned a withering gaze on the boy's mother. 'I shall have to speak to the captain about this, I think. Small boys don't dine with their elders and betters like this!' She gave a derisory sniff and Fiona curbed an overwhelming impulse to kick out at the brocaded legs under the table. The situation, however, was saved by Tommy himself, who pulled himself up into a rigid sitting position and declared loudly:

'I think I *would* like a good supper after all!'

There was a sudden splutter of mirth from Sandra, a noise which ceased abruptly as the vast bosom swayed while its owner turned to inspect her, distaste making the sulky face thoroughly unpleasant. What might have been said remained unsaid because Mrs Bottlin-Mabee's eyes suddenly caught the movement of two men approaching their table. Immediately her face became wreathed in smiles and she began to simper.

'It's Captain Howard *at last*. Captain! Cooee!'

The tall man accompanying Doctor Maynard paused, hurriedly hid his dismay and then walked leisurely across to the table. Before he had reached it, a plump, ringed hand was clutching his, squeezing and mauling it.

'Oh, Captain, how absolutely delightful to see you again! You remember me, of course? From last year, when we went to Alicante and Lebanon. Mrs Edith Bottlin-Mabee, *the* furniture widow, you know.'

'Ah yes, how could I possibly forget?' Alan Howard replied in a suave tone. 'Is everything to your satisfaction?'

'No,' came the pouting reply. 'I wanted to be at your table, but the doctor here,' she beamed at Dr Maynard, her eyes almost vanishing beneath the fleshy folds around them, 'he explained that it was his turn to honour me. All the same,' she lowered her voice to a whisper, 'perhaps I could see you in your cabin later? I have something important and private that I'd like to discuss with you.'

Throughout this conversation, Fiona had remained riveted in her seat, her clasped hands cold and clammy. Her heart was pounding like a sledge hammer, for this man was the Alan Howard to whom she had been engaged. She had seen him approach head and shoulders above the man at his side, a slight greying of hair at the temple, and with more lines than she cared to see on his handsome face. There were little crows-feet of strain about the eyes and his mouth was set in a hard, tight line. She watched him bend over the effusive Mrs Bottlin-Mabee, heard his voice trying to placate her, and waited for him to look up and see that she was here. But had he known already, she wondered.

'You ladies are comfortable?' he asked at last, straightening to glance first at Sandra and then at Fiona. Her heart stopped. The eyes were uninterested. For all he cared, she could have been a complete stranger. He showed no pleasure at seeing her; if anything, his gaze was openly hostile. The moment did not last long, for he bent to speak to Tommy.

'So you've had measles, eh? Nasty things. I had them when I was about your age. Mind you eat well. Tomorrow you'll find plenty of things to do with the other youngsters on board. Now may I bid you all good evening and say that I hope you will find your first dinner satisfactory?'

There were murmurs from all but Mrs Bottlin-Mabee who seemed determined to detain the captain, but he firmly walked away without a backward glance. Fiona watched and saw him go to a table standing less than ten yards from their own. When he sat down he was facing her, yet he did not seek to look directly at her.

There was a good choice for dinner, but somehow Fiona had lost her appetite. She drank less than half her cream of asparagus soup, refused the plaice tartare, and ate very little of the roast chicken chasseur. But the ice cream was good, she thought, sadly chasing a morsel of broken wafer around the bottom of the dish with her spoon.

When they had finished dinner, Sandra announced that she would prefer to spend the remainder of the evening before she went to bed in the library, choosing one or two books. Fiona accompanied her to the comfortably furnished room forward on the lounge deck. The only other occupants were an elderly couple; the man was deep in a newspaper, while his wife searched briskly through the shelves of light reading for one of her favourite romantic authors, accompanying her mission with a gasp of delight.

'Just fancy, Jack, here's the book I was trying to get from our local library . . .' and 'Well, I never, and it's been out of print all these years!' Her husband greeted these remarks with gruff sounds from behind the newspaper. Fiona winked at Sandra and moved to the crime shelf, hoping to find an Agatha Christie.

The two girls spent a contented half-hour in the library, where Fiona came to the conclusion that she would never be at a loss for good reading material while aboard ship. As they walked slowly back to their cabin, Sandra said:

'Just because I'm having an early night, please don't think you have to as well. Why don't you go to one of the bars and have a drink? Or the ship's cinema, perhaps.'

'As a matter of fact,' Fiona replied, tapping the shiny book cover, 'I think I'd like to start this. As long as you don't mind my bedhead light on for a little while?'

'Of course not. Read as long as you like and forget about me.'

Fiona's plan, however, was not carried out. They had been back at their cabin for less than five minutes when there came a knock on the door. Fiona opened it to find a steward outside.

'Miss Barclay?'

'Yes.'

'The captain's compliments, but could you spare him half an hour, please? He would like to speak to you in his cabin.'

Fiona's hand flew to her throat where she was sure a pulse beat visibly. She was conscious of Sandra's interested gaze behind her. She coughed awkwardly.

'Er . . . *now*?'

'If you please, miss, although the captain asks me to say that if tomorrow morning would be more convenient, then he could see you at nine-forty-five.'

'No, I'll come now. But where do I go, and how can I find my way?'

'I'm to escort you, miss.'

'Oh, thank you. If you wouldn't mind waiting a few minutes, please, while I get ready?'

'Of course, miss. I'll be at the far end of the corridor.'

'Thank you.' Fiona closed the door, her hand shaking. She drew a deep breath before turning to face her companion.

'Well!' Sandra chuckled. 'Whatever does our illustrious captain want, I wonder? He didn't seem anything beyond the ordinary limit of the politeness one would expect from such a lofty personage when he greeted us during dinner.' She wrinkled her brow, watching Fiona who had bent over the bed where her handbag lay, rummaging inside it, ostensibly for a handkerchief. Her cheeks were hot and she knew Sandra must see her discomfort.

'I expect it could be something to do with you,' Fiona ventured in what she hoped to be a casual tone. 'You know, just out of hospital, and still under the wing of the medics.'

'Well, I don't! Special attention from the doctor himself—yes, I can understand that. But not from the captain, who I'm sure has far better things to do than to dally with each member on the passenger list. I sense intrigue here. Could you unzip me before you go, please? It seems to have jammed up at the neck.' Her hands were at the back of her head and Fiona moved to her to sort out the muddle of light fabric which had caught in the zip's teeth. She wrestled gently and then slid the zip open.

Sandra yawned.

'Thanks. I shall be waiting to hear all about it when you come back.'

'There might be difficulty because I'm a last-minute passenger,' Fiona suggested.

'I doubt it. Everything was sorted out before we left, otherwise they'd never have allowed you to board. Thanks for unzipping me. I'll take a shower before turning in.'

Fiona dashed a pink lipstick across her mouth, picked up her handbag and reached for a cardigan before leaving the cabin and joining the steward whom she found waiting as promised.

'This way, miss.'

It seemed to Fiona that they traversed miles of corridors passing public rooms en route, went up lifts and then down more corridors before reaching the officers' quarters near the bridge on the boat deck. Gone was all the luxury of the public parts of the ship. Accommodation here was simple and practical, without unnecessary furbelows. The steward paused outside a varnished timber door on which a notice proclaimed:

Captain.

Fiona's hands felt clammy. Hastily she took the handkerchief from her handbag and wiped her palms before pushing the article away again. The steward knocked, opened the door and announced:

'Miss Barclay, sir,' before stepping aside to allow Fiona entrance.

The cabin was of reasonable size, well-lit but austere. Plainly it was a day cabin, because a large desk took up most of the room, although there were comfortable armchairs set before an electric fire. Fiona noticed very little of her surroundings, however, when her eyes fell on Alan, who was seated behind the desk. He had discarded his uniform coat and the strong light hanging above seemed to glare in a brittle fashion off the white shirt he wore. She did not notice the steward's withdrawal until the cabin door was shut behind him, leaving her alone with Alan. His face bore no trace of welcome, and his mouth was set in a firm line. She swallowed, her fingers tightening over the top of her handbag. Alan stood up and placed a chair for her. His arm almost brushed hers and she felt a swift tingle of fear, and something else.

Alan returned to the far side of the desk, dropped his large frame into it in the familiar flowing motion she had come to associate with him, and then clasped his hands together, placing them on the mahogany desktop in front of him. Her eyes were drawn to those big, strong knuckles ... she suddenly wished she had refused his invitation. Yet had it been one? Surely more of an order than a request!

'I see you're well,' he said, breaking the silence at last.

'Yes, thank you.'

'I thought we should get one matter clear from the very start. I have no intention of bringing up the past, no matter what you did three years ago.' His eyes flashed like cold metal, sending a shiver of fear through her. She had to look away. 'Yes, I expect you *do* feel guilty! However, that's all water under the bridge, as they say. You wanted nothing more to do with me. And I, a short time later, decided I had nothing further to say to you. Our parting became a mutual blessing, and one for which now I'm trebly thankful.' Fiona winced. His words and tone cut deeply. If only ... but he was speaking again and she felt compelled to listen.

'Naturally I see the passenger lists before sailing and the name of Barclay registered with me. I have had Barclays before, but never a Miss Fiona. However, I thought it might be one of those coincidences, but unfortunately it was not. Why you chose this ship is immaterial to me, also whether you knew I was her captain. However, if you've come aboard hoping to ... what shall we call it? ... "patch things up", perhaps? ...'

He got no further. Fiona pushed back her chair and rose to her feet, her cheeks flushed with anger.

'I don't have to stay here and be insulted by *you*!' she flared at him. 'Just to get the record straight, *Captain* Howard, had I known you were on this ... this thing ... then I certainly shouldn't have sailed with her.' So there! her tone plainly implied.

His mouth twisted into an unkind smile.

'Sit down, will you? I haven't finished. What I have to say to you in private is between ourselves but I intend to finish, even if I have to hold you here by force.'

Fiona sank back into her chair, tears sparkling in her fine eyes, but he appeared quite impervious to the effect he was having on her. She hoped she would not cry in front of him! She felt so weak, so totally unsure of herself ... just as she had felt those few days before the wedding that never took place. What was wrong with her? She was afraid of him! Afraid, yet fascinated by the power of his magnetism. His shirt gleamed whitely and she could see the ripple of muscles beneath it, and the darkening patches where chest hair grew. Oh, how wonderful it would be could she just throw herself at him, her arms about his waist, and weep out the misery of these past three years!

He was speaking once more.

'You're on this ship for fourteen days. We have to live on the confines of this "little island", as one might say. This liner is not what we all vulgarly term a "banana boat", so my duties as a captain are totally different from those I used to have while commanding the small freighter. I have to look at a cruise in a certain light. Each passenger is a "guest" and, as captain, it is only right and correct that I accord each and every one the utmost politeness and courtesy. Even should I take exception to someone, I'm not allowed to show my dislike. I'm obliged to be very civil, or I shouldn't be in the position I am. The captain of a liner like this has to be firmly in command of his officers and crew, and a diplomat where the passengers are concerned. Now do you understand? Look at me, please!' She forced herself to meet those hard eyes which bored mercilessly into hers. 'Fortunately only the four walls of this cabin can hear what I'm saying to you now, so any lapse on my part goes unreported to my employers. Fiona, had I the option, I assure you I wouldn't even acknowledge your presence on this ship!' She drew her breath in a little gasp, then winced. His expression changed fleetingly, but then the hardness was back. 'I'm not my own master, so I'm obliged to treat you with civility and courtesy, like all the rest of our passengers.'

Fire flamed up Fiona's throat and cheeks. Her eyes

burned as unshed tears threatened. She swallowed and managed to whisper in a small, but rigidly controlled voice:

'Is it necessary to humble me like this? You're very hurtful.'

He pushed back his chair and stood up, turning his back to her. After a short pause, he asked:

'Have I made myself clear?'

'Perfectly, thank you, Alan.' Her voice cut through the chilled atmosphere like a knife. 'I recognise that you dislike me intensely and, unpleasant as it must be for you to have me aboard, fourteen days is not a particularly long period. One, I'm sure, you'll manage to surmount with your customary aplomb. And believe me, I shan't lower myself to write a formal letter of complaint to the directors of this shipping line. May I now be shown the way back to my cabin, please? Everything is so strange and I certainly shouldn't like to get lost and embarrass you by turning up in a forbidden zone.'

She walked to the door, but he was beside her, his hand on her arm.

'I'll send for someone at once.'

'In the meantime,' she retorted, plucking off his hand as if his fingers were the clinging tentacles of an octopus, 'kindly refrain from touching me. I find you abhorrent!'

Within half a minute there came a knock at the door, but it was the longest half-minute of Fiona's life as she sat stonily in a chair while Alan selected a cigarette from a gold case, put it to his lips, and then lit it. With a tiny pang, she recognised the case. It was the one she had given him shortly before they had arranged the date of their wedding...

'Ah, Steward, kindly escort Miss Barclay back to the

main deck where she has her cabin. She'll tell you the number.' In the presence of the other man, he smiled at Fiona. 'May I wish you a good night, Miss Barclay? And thank you for sparing me your time.'

'Not at all, Captain. Believe me, it was a *pleasure.*' There was a heavy inflection of sarcasm on her final word, which did not go unnoticed by the steward whose eyes darted from one to the other of them. She felt a surge of triumph when she realised her shaft had hit its mark. A muscle was working in Alan's temple and there was a light in his eyes that confirmed her suspicion of the fury raging within him. She swept out of the cabin, her head high; when the door was shut behind her, a tremendous wave of unhappiness came over her, the triumph she had felt evaporating as if it had never been. She did not see the officer who approached, her tears were so blinding. Neither did she see his smile of greeting, followed quickly by a frown of puzzlement. Then Doctor Maynard knocked on Alan's door, receiving a curt and impatient order to come in.

It took a great deal of control to prevent the tears from falling. Fiona despised herself, especially for her weakness in the company of the steward. Suddenly she addressed him.

'I think I know my way from here, thank you. I've decided to take a short walk before turning in.'

'It will be cold on the promenade deck, miss,' he pointed out, and she held up the cardigan she had been carrying in her left hand.

'I shall be all right, Steward. Thank you, and goodnight.'

'Goodnight, miss.'

He held open a door on to the promenade deck. The

cool air hit Fiona like a draught of fresh spring water. After the initial gasp, she slid her arms quickly into the sleeves of her cardigan and began to walk slowly along the deck, listening to the swish of the water through which they were travelling and the far-off thrumming of the liner's powerful engines. There were not many other passengers on the promenade deck, so she chose a sheltered place near the rail, leaning her elbows on it and gazing out at the black sea. There was a tiny moon, a moon which shed a silver, phosphorescent light on rippling, moving waters that glittered in its light like metal straight from the foundry. The sight soon dimmed as the tears gathered and tumbled down her cheeks.

It had been a hateful, hateful interview! Alan had said some very cruel things to her. He did not want her here and was prepared to speak to her only because it was his duty. Duty! But had she not deserved every morsel of harsh treatment? Had she been in his shoes that day three years ago, how would *she* have felt? Alan's pride must have suffered a severe blow, and men were proud creatures. Do almost anything you liked to them, but never, never seek to destroy their pride! That was a well-known maxim. If only this voyage was on its last night! Thirteen more to live through. Nights when the knowledge of Alan's presence must torment and persecute her. Why could not he have agreed to forget past differences? Why seek her out to tell her deliberately that he hated her? Because that's what really lay at the bottom of that strange interview in his cabin just now. Why? *Why?*

'Am I disturbing you?' asked a voice at her elbow. She jumped and spun round to face the smiling face of the doctor. 'I'm sure that thin thing won't be sufficient to keep you warm for long.' He touched her cardigan, feeling its quality with his fingers. 'I know a doctor's lot is not a happy one, and we have many problems, but I'm sure I don't want to have to dose one of my passengers for such a simple thing as the common cold!'

Fiona managed a smile and fumbled in her handbag for her handkerchief. Turning her head away from him, she blew her nose and dabbed furtively at her eyes, hoping he would not notice tear-traces in this rather dim light.

'You're upset,' he remarked in a kind tone. 'Don't you feel well? I have seasickness remedies, if that's what's beginning to trouble you.'

'No, I'm perfectly all right,' she replied. 'I expect it's the wind out here making my eyes water. Perhaps I should go in.' She was loath to do so lest Sandra comment on her red eyes.

'Want a solid shoulder?' Dr Maynard asked. 'Something tells me you need one. Oh, by the way, we passed each other less than five minutes ago.'

'Oh! I'm sorry. Where?'

He coughed and leaned closer to say in a low voice:

'Outside our captain's cabin. And, if you don't mind my saying so, he was in a filthy mood. Almost threw the desk at me when I joined him.' This made her laugh, as he had intended. 'Now,' he began to trace the configuration of the rail with one finger, 'I know sufficient about shipboard life to realise that a captain always has to present a smiling, courteous face to all his passengers, even if he hates the shape of their ears, or can't stand the purple of their bejewelled bosoms. It's quite unlike Alan to lose his cool, just because an attractive ... and unattached ... young lady happened to have called on him. This useful appendage,' he tapped his rather long nose, 'which serves me in a great many capacities, tells me that all is not well between two people who are supposed ... *supposed*, please note ... to have met for the first time at dinner this evening. I surmise that these two people have known each other exceedingly well at some time in the past, and that their proximity on this liner is not to the particular liking of either.' He paused, his gaze resting on Fiona's bent head. Encouraged by her silence and lack of any rebuff, he continued: 'I've known Captain Howard for a long time, and what I haven't been told, I've been able to work out for myself. Could it be, I asked myself just now, that this very charming companion of a certain young widow in my care, is more than just a name to the captain? And, I ask myself once more, could it also be that he once felt deeply for the aforesaid young lady? Finally I ask myself: why has he picked a quarrel with her, or did she seek him out to throw herself at his head again and he's no longer interested?'

'Oh no!' Fiona retorted quickly. 'It wasn't like that at all. I mean ...' she bit her lip, realising she had given herself away. Dr Maynard's hand closed over hers.

'I understand, my dear. Perhaps more than either of you could possibly know. Seeing him again tonight has been a shock to you, because you didn't know he captained this ship.'

'No, I didn't, although I was forewarned on seeing his name. I was prepared when we went to dinner.'

'To you I expect I sound very interfering, but one thing I must know, because I can't have you suffering sleepless nights and unhappiness. Is this meeting going to cause emotional trouble for you?'

'How ... how do you mean?'

'Fourteen days are like eternity when you're in love with someone who wants nothing more to do with you.'

'I'm ... I'm not in love with him. Not now.'

'I see.' She could tell by his tone that he did not believe her and, she thought wryly, why on earth should he, because she wasn't sure she believed herself!

'But I shall be all right, I promise. I'm here to care for Sandra, and I won't let my personal feelings destroy her convalescence.'

'Good girl!' he said approvingly. 'But don't forget, if ever you feel in urgent need of that shoulder I promised, I'm always around somewhere.'

'What happened?' was Sandra's eager question when Fiona returned to their cabin. She was sitting up in bed, a pretty blue bedjacket tossed about her shoulders, and an open book in her hand. This she put down at once to study Fiona's rather drawn face. 'Is something wrong? You look awful.'

'I'm all right, thank you.'

Sandra hugged her knees, asking:

'Tell me all about it! I've been dying for you to come back. What's he like when you get him alone? Or was someone else with you both?'

Fiona turned away her face so that her companion should not see her expression.

'He ... he was polite and ... and ...' She was at a total loss for words.

'And?' Sandra prompted

Fiona suddenly made up her mind. She came over to her friend's bed and sat down on it with rather a bump. The book slid to the cabin floor, but she made no attempt to pick it up.

'Listen, Sandra, I'd better put you in the picture. You see, Alan Howard and I were once good friends.' Sandra's eyes widened. 'Even more than good friends, but it just didn't work out. Believe me, had I known he would be in charge of this ship, I'd never have agreed to come.'

'Then I'm glad you didn't know, otherwise where would I be now?' There was a hint of laughter in the other girl's tone.

'I'm sorry, that was rude of me. Of course I'd have come. It was just so unexpected meeting him again. The last time ... all those years ago ... he captained a very much smaller cargo vessel, and I certainly wouldn't have dreamed of such a step-up in the world.'

Shrewdly Sandra asked:

'Is that why it failed, perhaps?'

Fiona coloured.

'No. His position, or climbing the social ladder, wasn't important. We just couldn't hit it off.'

'And he wanted to tell you that he'd like to be friends again, is that the reason for your visit to the cabin?'

'No. The opposite, as a matter of fact. He explained his position and how difficult it would be to treat me with anything other than common courtesy ...'

'So you weren't to feel embarrassed at all, because he wouldn't be doing anything awful like cutting you dead in front of a crowd. Is that what he said?'

Fiona sighed thankfully.

'Yes, more or less. I was to treat him just as the captain, and everything would be all right.'

'And that satisfies you, too?'

'Of course.'

Sandra leaned closer, her eyes gentle.

'Then why the face of gloom and despondency, eh? Does the lady protest too much, perhaps, or whatever the saying is? Can it be that somewhere deep down you still hold a tiny flickering torch for him?'

Fiona had found an intense interest in the shape of a cuticle, lifting her hand and twisting it to and fro so that a better light fell on it.

'I don't exactly hate him, Sandra,' she replied in a whisper. 'Not as vehemently as he appears to hate me.'

The other girl sank back against her pillows.

'Oh dear!' she sighed sadly. 'Then it was much, much more than the "just good friends" type of relationship. And the hurt still smarts. Tell me, or am I probing too deeply, how long ago did it happen?'

'A little over three years.'

'And you haven't seen each other since?'

'No.'

There was a long pause. Finally Sandra broke it by suggesting in a bright and brisk voice:

'Plenty long enough to heal the wounds! What you now have to do is to look forward and forget about the past. You're here to enjoy yourself and if that Captain Alan Whatsisname is going to upset you, then I shall have something to say, too! I'm convalescent, remember? If I catch you glancing over your shoulder at all those skeletons happily rattling their bones in the past, I shall have to take drastic measures. Although what I'm not sure at the moment. So ...' she laid a soft hand on Fiona's and squeezed it, 'forget the hurt. Try to see him as he is: the very efficient captain of the liner on which we've chosen to spend a fortnight's perfect cruise! Who knows, by the end of it, you may even be able to see him in a much more favourable light and step ashore with the firm conclusion that he's one ghost you've well and truly laid for good! Agreed?'

'I'll try. I suppose I feel a little strange at the moment because it's the first time for so long that we've been alone together. He put his cards on the table; gave me more or less my instructions, and now we both know what's expected. And I promise not to allow my own feelings to spoil our fun here.'

Surprisingly, Fiona slept fairly well, although her mind was reliving those moments with Alan just before she fell asleep. Twice during the night the low thrumming of far-distant engines awoke her, but she managed to forget their presence and drift off again. When she was aroused by the arrival of their cabin stewardess the following morning, she was grateful for the early morning tea-tray. She poured two cups and handed one to Sandra, who confessed that she had never slept better. The curtains were pulled back from the window and, to their delight, the sky beyond was blue and the sun shone pleasantly. Instead of partaking of a continental breakfast in their cabin, they decided to go to the dining-room and eat there. The room was almost empty, most of the passengers having preferred to remain in their cabins with the luxury of breakfast in bed. There was one other occupant of their table: young Tommy, who grinned a welcome as he continued to tuck into fried egg and bacon while Fiona ordered rolls and coffee.

'Is your mother coming?' she asked.

'No. They're sick. Auntie felt sick last night as Mum said, but they're both moaning about the way this boat rolls. But she doesn't, does she? The boat, I mean?' More bacon was crammed into the eager mouth. 'I don't feel it, do you?'

Both girls shook their heads.

'As a matter of fact,' Sandra smiled back, 'I was only thinking on my way here to the dining-room that the sea was remarkably flat.'

'That's the stabilisers, you see. I know all about them

because I learned quite a bit about ships and things before we came. Stops the boat rolling about too much and makes it more comfortable for the people aboard. Anyway, I'm glad in a way that Mum and Auntie are still in their bunks. I can explore the ship on my own without being told not to go here and not to go there.' A frown pukered his brow. 'It *will* be all right, won't it? I hope so, because I don't know anyone here very well yet.'

'We'll ask the steward what to do about it,' Fiona suggested. 'I expect he'll tell you where to go, although it's probably the purser's job to organise excursions.'

'Mum said there's one for the adults, you know—excursion about the ship. She said we can look over at it at certain times when the crew isn't busy, but she won't want to go down to the engine rooms. I do, because I love engines and things that work. I want to go on the bridge and see the captain. I hope that's also allowed. Do you think it is? And should I ask him?'

The girls exchanged a glance.

'I'm afraid neither of us can pass judgement on that particular matter,' Sandra ventured, 'but the purser would know.'

'Good. I know where his office is, because Mum wanted to leave her pearls in the safe last night.' Tommy grinned. 'They're not very valuable, really, but Mum's fond of them and she'd be terribly upset if someone pinched them from her. Do you think people would do any stealing aboard this ship?' he finished anxiously.

'Tommy, whenever you get a large gathering of people, and whatever you think about their honesty, there's usually someone who isn't as honest as you might be. It's very unfortunate, but one of those things which can't be ignored. Therefore, because there is just this one ... or maybe two

... the rest of us are sensible to take simple precautions. Never put temptation in anyone's way because even the strongest of us can fall, depending on what that particular temptation is. Your mother is wise to have her pearls locked away. Maybe their monetary value is low in the eyes of the world, but if she's fond of them, then they're absolutely beyond price to her. Do you understand what I'm saying?'

'Oh yes. Sentimental value, that's what you're getting at, isn't it. Like burglars. It's not what they take that really matters; it's the useless little things they might break or spoil simply because they can't find value in them for themselves. Now, I've finished my breakfast, so would you mind if I left the table, please? I'll ask that steward over there. 'Bye!' He stood up and almost ran from the dining-room. Sandra laughed.

'Poor kid! I hope he can find friends of his own age aboard. Travelling with a seasick mum and aunt can't be much fun for the child. But the bridge! wow! Knowing your captain as you do, would such a visit be permitted?'

Fiona shrugged.

'I couldn't even hazard a guess, although I expect he might take the trouble to explain how everything works to someone who's obviously as interested as Tommy.'

As she buttered a crisp roll, Sandra remarked blithely:

'You could always ask for Tommy, couldn't you? After all, you know the man. Why don't you make use of him while you're here?'

For a moment Fiona said nothing, then she tossed her head and replied:

'I might possibly consider it, if we happen to get into conversation, which I greatly doubt, but I'm certainly not deliberately seeking him out!' Her cheeks had reddened although the tinge began to fade when she smiled. 'Surely you've seen sufficient of young Tommy to realise that once he sets his mind on something he'll probably succeed in getting it, by hook or by crook? When I saw him at dinner last night, I thought he was rather sat-on and lacking in character, but this morning I've changed my mind. He seems to have found his feet.'

'The timely absence of his fond mama, perhaps?' Sandra suggested with a knowing wink, and they both laughed.

They discussed their plans for the morning, with Sandra suggesting that Fiona might care to sign her name for deck games. The latter shook her head.

'Not at the moment. I don't feel in the least active. I might decide later, after our call in Lisbon, perhaps. If you've no objection, I thought of being thoroughly lazy on deck, in a nice chair with a good book. The rush of the past week is beginning to tell well and truly. Besides, it's Sunday, the weather is fine, the sea flat and we're heading for warmer climes. Finally, I have a book I want to read.'

Shortly before ten both girls had established themselves in comfortable chairs on the sun terrace, out of the wind, and with the sun shining pleasantly on their faces. Already some of the hardier passengers were preparing to take a quick dip in the ship's swimming pool. Fiona watched them for a few minutes, then turned her attention to the novel she had borrowed from the reading-room.

'Good morning, ladies.' A voice spoke from their right, and both girls looked round hastily to find the doctor studying them with considerable amusement. He chuckled aloud and then drew up another chair, parking himself beside them at such an angle that he could see them properly.

'I trust you'll forgive me for resting my feet for just two

minutes,' he continued. 'For first day out, I seem to have had a surprisingly large number of folk on my sick list, mostly the symptoms of the inevitable *mal de mer*. Are you feeling all right, Mrs Stern?'

'Thank you, yes. I find the motion of the ship quite pleasurable. And I have an exciting book.'

'I hope that remark doesn't mean that I've interrupted you at the wrong moment, because believe me, I shall be heartbroken.' His eyes smiled warmly at her and, to Fiona's delighted interest, a tiny blush stole into Sandra's cheeks. She interrupted the exchange to invite him to share coffee with them.

'I was just about to suggest we catch the steward's eye and ordered some,' she continued. 'Do stay. I'm sure you aren't needed in the sick bay. In any case, you can inspect one of your patients quite happily as you enjoy her company over coffee,' she finished on a smile.

The coffee was brought very quickly and Dr Maynard passed round the plate of delicious-looking biscuits which had been included on the tray. Fiona pulled a face before shrugging and biting deeply into a thick shortbread.

'You know what they say,' she sighed, 'forty seconds in the mouth, forty years on the hips.'

'And very nice hips they are too!' the doctor scolded. 'Some of you women and your fads about weight! You're on holiday, so enjoy yourselves. There'll be plenty of time to measure the inches once you're back home. Mrs Stern?'

'Please call me Sandra,' she reminded him with a gentle smile. He pulled his chair a little closer and leaned across to pick up her book. 'In that case, I'm Robert. Good yarn, that,' he remarked, replacing the book carefully, but not before Fiona noticed that his fingers had brushed Sandra's. It was a very casual gesture, yet Fiona was convinced that it held great significance for them both. She looked away, suddenly unable to bear the moment of someone else's shared intimacy. The swimming pool was empty now, but a figure was approaching from its starboard side. Her hand rose slowly to her throat.

How magnificent Alan looked in his uniform! she thought, as sun glinted on gold braid. She watched him pause to address each passenger, and caught their welcoming smiles. Would he come over here, or would he pass to the lower deck before reaching them?

Alan made no sign that he had seen Fiona on the sun terrace and she was afraid that her fears would be realised; that he would not come her way. Robert Maynard, however, provided the solution by standing up, the movement drawing Alan's attention to the small group.

'Thank you for the coffee,' Robert said, his back to the approaching captain. 'I hope to see you both at lunch. Unless you're planning to have it on deck in the sun?'

'We ...' Sandra began hesitantly, her eyes seeking Fiona's. She was about to say that they had not yet decided what to do when Alan's voice broke into the conversation.

'Good morning—Mrs Stern, isn't it? I trust you slept well and are enjoying your first day at sea?'

'Yes, thank you, Captain.'

'And you, Miss Barclay?' His gaze locked with hers, but there was no friendliness in it. Sandra exchanged a hasty glance with Robert, who was frowning rather heavily.

'Very well, thank you, Captain. And why shouldn't I? I have no worries or troubles.'

'I'm glad.' Now he appeared bored with her, turning instead to bend over Sandra. 'Have you everything you want? A rug for your knees, perhaps? Just ask the steward and he'll attend to you at once.'

'I'm perfectly all right, Captain,' she responded a little shyly. He looked so big, towering over her like that, but there was an attractive lilt to his voice that set her wondering whatever could have happened to make him dislike Fiona so much. That he did dislike her had been brought home very forcibly just now. She had felt him bristle with it almost, she thought, and there had been real hardness in his eyes when they had looked at poor Fiona. Yet she seemed to be bearing up very well under it. If his attitude hurt, the pain was being well hidden.

'Oh God!' she heard Robert's faint whisper beside her and gave him a swift, puzzled look. He indicated the plump figure bustling towards them along the terrace. 'I'll see you later,' he said to Sandra, but Mrs Bottlin-Mabee was already upon them all. Her face was wreathed in smiles, the large mouth a slash of vermilion—just like a fresh cut in meat, Fiona thought.

'Oh, Captain Howard, how are you this morning? *Just* the person I wanted to see. I don't know what people are coming to these days, but the top window in my cabin jammed and the man who came to put it right just doesn't seem to know his job. Could you take a look at it for me, please?' One plump arm slid through his, while she twisted her head at an uncomfortable angle in order to gush up at him. 'I'll have coffee brought to my cabin for us both.'

Alan politely detached his arm, saying in a calm tone:

'I regretfully must decline your offer of coffee, Mrs Bottlin-Mabee. And I'm distressed to hear of the trouble with your window. However, as you know already, it's the purser's province, not mine. Dr Maynard, just a moment before you sli ...' he sounded as if he was about to say 'slink off' but corrected himself in time. Robert halted.

'Before you return to the sick bay, would you be so kind as to escort this good lady to the purser's office? Thank you. And now, ladies,' this almost in the same breath, 'I'll leave you to your leisure.' He smiled gently at Sandra, avoided Fiona's eyes completely, and strode away. The reluctant Robert towed his unwanted companion in the opposite direction.

CHAPTER THREE

It was Monday evening, the day before the liner was due to arrive at Lisbon. The atmosphere at the doctor's table was gay and carefree and tonight even Tommy's mother and rather quiet, mousey aunt appeared to have blossomed out, joining with the general conversation. Tommy himself was absent, having taken himself off to another table to eat with a new-found friend.

The passengers had been at sea for a few days and various friendships were being forged. With the zest and vigour of childhood, Tommy had found himself a firm friend who ate at a table not very far from the doctor's. During the daytime, the two boys were rarely apart and the separation at meals had proved irksome to them both. Tommy's mother had insisted that this wonderful new friendship somehow would survive even if they had to eat apart, but the demands of her son proved too much for her. An almost continuous system of winks and arm signals was set up between the two boys so that neither should eat what the other did not. They were going through the phase in which everything they did must be identical, even down to the brand of toothpaste each used. Their respective dining tables were not close enough to allow conversation but sufficiently distant to permit of signalling. Robert Maynard watched these proceedings with a twinkle in his eye, until one of Tommy's more vehement signals sent a heavily laden tray crashing out of the arms of a waitress who happened to be passing at that very moment. While the mess was being cleared from the floor, and Tommy receiving the lash of both his mother's and his aunt's tongues, Robert quietly suggested that a compromise might be found. After a great deal of discussion following on the meal, it was decided that Tommy should dine at his friend's table, and his friend take breakfast at the doctor's. However, at the first inkling of bad behaviour or disobedience, this arrangement would be terminated forthwith.

Sandra had made friends with a young married couple called Walters who ate at the doctor's table and, during dinner, they discussed what to do the following day.

'We're hoping to go ashore, naturally,' Peter Walters remarked, helping himself from the cheese board and selecting a large slice of Gouda. 'How about you and Fiona? Were you planning to see Lisbon too?'

'Yes,' Sandra replied. 'I know we won't have very long, but it seems a pity to miss the opportunity!'

'Why don't we all go together?' Julia Walters suggested after a glance at her husband. 'It would be such fun. What do you think?'

The idea was readily agreed upon and the talk continued on these lines; at the first opportunity Fiona asked Robert whether he was allowed to go ashore whenever they reached port.

'We have a duty rota, depending on what's to be done here. Fortunately I have very few patients in the sick bay ... just one, to be exact ... so I can allow my deputy time off tomorrow. We usually try to share and share alike. During the last cruise, I had time in Lisbon and he did not. Now it's his turn. If we have many patients, then neither of us goes ashore, not even for one or two hours. You should have an enjoyable trip,' he finished.

Fiona's eyes strayed towards the captain's table. Alan

was leaning attentively towards the woman who sat on his right, his brown head bent slightly, and she saw him nod. She envied that woman, yet why should she? If she were there in her place, the atmosphere would lose its warmth and friendliness . . . and she her appetite.

Alan finished dinner before them. Fiona could not help watching him as he rose to his feet, pulled out the chair of the woman who had sat next to him, waited for her to precede him, and then strode in a leisurely fashion from the dining saloon, without even so much as a glance in Fiona's direction. She bit her lower lip, hastily looking away. Robert watched her thoughtfully and lightly began to tap the tablecloth with his fingers.

In company with the Walters, Fiona and Sandra took coffee in the lounge, after which they all repaired to the ship's cinema and laughed themselves silly over a hilarious send-up of a Western which none of them had seen before. The atmosphere in the cinema was very smoky and hot; Fiona was thankful to leave it after the film had ended. Peter suggested a nightcap in the bar, but when they reached it they found it very crowded and just as smoky as the cinema they had vacated.

'It's a warm night,' Peter said. 'Let's sit on deck for a while and I'll bring the drinks there.'

'Find a steward, darling,' Julia replied. 'After all, it's his job, not yours.' Peter merely smiled and vanished among the crush of people inside the bar. The three girls wandered on to the deck and found four empty chairs for themselves. The lighting on deck was mellow and warm, giving the ship an air of soft tropical mystery even though she was far away from the tropics. The coloured bulbs swung gently with the forward motion and the boisterous sound of the latest pop song wafted out from the dance floor next door to the bar.

Julia began describing her experiences of the lifeboat drill which they all had undergone during their first day out.

'Of course we knew it couldn't be for real, so we didn't bother to hurry. Pete was in the shower, so he decided to get dressed and take his time. We've seen lifeboat drills on the films and everyone seems to rush about in panic, screeching and shrieking, so we thought we'd wait until everyone else had gone. Mind you,' she laughed, 'had the ship really been in danger, I expect we'd have gone to the bottom pretty promptly! Anyway, when we finally got to our allotted station, the officer in charge was in quite a tizzy and the captain was also there, checking on us all, I think. Did he come and check you?' she asked Fiona.

'No, I don't think so. Although he could have done so when I went below again to collect our lifejackets. We'd been on deck in any case, so there wasn't far for us to go, but no jackets, so I went back again. Did he come round, Sandra, because you didn't mention it if he did?'

'No, although I thought I saw him in the distance.'

'Well, as I was saying, he gave Pete and me a pretty hard stare, just as if we were naughty kids! And I don't know what he said on the quiet to our officer, because the poor chap went brick red. Pete wanted to buy him a drink afterwards, but he told us he was still on duty and would have to decline. Ah, here is Peter with some very welcome sustenance.'

Fiona found the long cooling drink absolutely delicious; she sipped it slowly, her thoughts far away while the other three continued to talk amongst themselves.

'I liked the bit where the cavalry charged through the Indians as they chased that officer, and the Indians swung aside to let them through!' Sandra chuckled, reliving again an amusing moment in the film.

A familiar figure approached along the deck and Fiona's hand tightened around the base of the tall glass. Alan was dressed in evening mess dress, a uniform which enhanced his good looks in a devastating manner, especially now that the soft rays of light from the swinging bulbs blurred away the lines of hardness on his face. Inwardly Fiona moaned, unable to control the desperate longing which had begun to rise within her. She knew she was acting stupidly, allowing physical yearnings to swamp reason.

He paused and came to their group where he started to exchange pleasantries with Peter. Fiona knew she could stand no more. She had to escape his magnetic presence or else give in to temptation, flinging herself into his arms to beg forgiveness for her actions of three years ago.

'Excuse me,' she choked, rising in haste to her feet. 'I . . . I must fetch a clean handkerchief.'

'Don't go,' Julia began. 'I have a spare, if you'd just wait.' But her offer fell on deaf ears as Fiona rushed away. Peter stared after her in astonishment while Alan's mouth hardened.

As Fiona reached the big doors, a couple were emerging on to the deck, the man having pushed back the door to a closed position. Fiona made a grab for it before it was completely shut, and misjudged the distance. Her fingers caught at the steel edge, clawing frantically, and then were squeezed hard between door and jamb. She let out a shrill cry of agony as the knuckles were crushed by the door's weight. The couple spun round. Voices rose in excited comment. People hurried to Fiona as she collapsed, moaning, on to the deck. She was oblivious to all but the excruciating pain in her hand and the great waves of blackness which were beginning to engulf her.

'Let me take her!' Alan's voice said as he crouched

beside her. Vaguely she heard his voice, but connected it with no one. She smelled the faint tang of tobacco and the pleasant aroma of a male toilet preparation which was annoyingly familiar yet to which she was unable to put a name. She leaned thankfully against the jacket of the man who held her and felt his breath fan her forehead. They were discussing her plight, that she knew, but what they said did not register above the stabbing pain.

'Is she badly hurt?' Sandra asked.

'Handkerchief, please.'

'Take mine.'

Fiona moaned as white linen was folded very gently about her bleeding fingers.

'I'm trying not to hurt you.' Alan looked up at Peter who was hovering close to them. 'Ring the sick bay, will you, and tell them to get the doctor. We'll get her down there.'

'I can carry her,' Peter replied, as the man who had come through the door before Fiona seized it announced that he would do the telephoning.

'Very well. When you get there, tell the doctor I'll be along later.' Alan relinquished his hold of Fiona as Peter's arms slid about her body.

'Can you walk, love?' the latter asked gently. Fiona managed to nod. 'Good. Julia, take her other side, will you?' But there was no need. Fiona was assisted to her feet, but Peter took most of her weight, guiding her skilfully along the deck towards the doors which would lead them eventually to the sick bay.

'What's happened?'

'What's wrong with her?' whispered the passengers they passed on the way. 'Has there been an accident?'

In the sick bay, a white-coated nurse awaited their arrival and immediately took charge, ushering Fiona and

Peter towards the examination couch where the former was covered with a thick blanket. The nurse took one look at the injured hand, tutted to herself and then kindly but firmly advised Fiona's companion that there was nothing more they could do until after she had been seen by the doctor.

'You two go back and finish your drinks,' Sandra suggested. 'I'll stay here with Fiona.' Peter and his wife departed while Sandra helped herself to a chair and sat down beside Fiona. She took the uninjured hand in her own and held it. This gesture made Fiona cry.

'That's right, dear, go ahead and cry as much as you like. It must hurt like the very devil.'

Robert appeared a short time later and Sandra stood up, lifting the chair out of his way. He asked what had happened and she told him. The nurse brought in a dressing trolley and the examination began.

'I think you've been lucky,' he said at last, smiling down into Fiona's wet eyes. 'Badly crushed, but no bones broken. Would you like me to X-ray them just to be sure, or shall we wait until the morning? Does this hurt?' He moved the fingers very carefully.

'Sore.'

'Not sharp pain?'

'No.'

'Good. A dressing for the night and I'll see you first thing tomorrow morning. No, when you return from Lisbon.'

'I don't feel like going anywhere at the moment,' she muttered.

'I'm sure you don't. I'll give you some pain-killer and you're to have a good night's rest. The hand will be pretty painful tomorrow, I expect, but there's no reason why you shouldn't go ashore as originally planned.' He turned to the nurse. 'Rustle up a cup of hot, sweet tea, will you?'

'Yes, sir.'

The torn skin was cleaned and dressings applied.

'You should keep this arm in a sling for a couple of days until the pain eases.' Deft fingers fastened the cumbersome dressings and Fiona managed a faint smile of thanks. The sharp pain had ebbed, leaving behind a dull, thudding ache which beat hard with her pulse. 'Feeling better now?'

'A little, thank you.'

'Good. Ah, here's Nurse with your tea. Let me help you to sit up.' The nurse placed the tray on a table and then moved to the couch to adjust the head controls so that Fiona was now in a supported sitting position. Robert handed her the cup. She was still shaking badly and his fingers helped steady it for her. 'Sip it slowly, then it'll do you more good. At the moment you're suffering from shock, so I want you to stay here and not rush back to your cabin until the trembling has gone.'

'Am I intruding?' a voice asked from behind them. Alan stood in the doorway of the examination room. 'How is the invalid?'

Robert bestowed an enquiring gaze upon the newcomer and then stepped away from the couch.

'I've finished all I had to do for the moment. Sandra, if you'll come with me, I'll give you the pain-killer I want Fiona to take just before she goes to bed.' He took the girl's arm, ushering her from the room and closing the door quietly behind him.

'If you've come to gloat, then you can go away again!' Fiona said with considerable spirit.

'I haven't,' was the calm response. 'I was concerned about your injury.'

'Oh? Why? Nothing personal, of course. I suppose you're afraid I might sue your shipping line for damages,' she remarked spitefully, then sipped the scalding tea. Alan shrugged.

'That's your prerogative, but you may not win. It could be said that you brought your injury upon yourself, rushing off like that for no reason at all. Sheer carelessness.'

'Thanks!'

'Not at all.'

There was a long silence during which Fiona studied the surface of the liquid in her cup. She knew he was looking at her but was afraid to meet his eye.

'Well?' she asked impatiently. 'What are you staying here for? You've seen that I'm bandaged up and will mend in time. Haven't you anything else to do on the bridge, or wherever it is you have to be at this time of night?'

He eased himself more comfortably into the chair recently vacated by Sandra and a mocking smile lurked at the corner of his mouth.

'Bad-tempered little bitch, aren't you? Can't you recognise genuine kindness when you meet it?'

'I don't *want* you here!' she retorted in anger. 'I just don't want you anywhere around me. Just as you told me you didn't want me!'

'So there!' he finished for her. She stared at him.

'So there what?'

'Just completing the usual childish remark. Go ahead, throw the cup at me if it'll make you feel any better,' he jibed as her mouth turned down. He stood up. 'Honestly, Fiona my love, you never seem to grow up, do you? Here am I, doing my captain's duty by making all the right solicitous noises about the injury caused to one of my passengers, while you sit and sulk, wondering whether to cause a second accident by chucking hot tea over me.' He raised a finger in warning. 'But if you *do*, my sweet, *I* shall sue *you*!'

Her tear-filled eyes met his and one spilled over.

'Oh, God!' he sighed, plunging a hand into a pocket to withdraw a clean handkerchief. 'Why must women always cry when they get the worst of any argument? Here, wipe your eyes.'

'I *hate* you!'

'Stale news, pet. I became very much aware of the fact more than three years ago.' He leaned over her, his face suddenly hard and cold. 'And what's more, do you believe me when I say I didn't like it one bit? Used to it now, of course. Time's a good healer ... for all kinds of things, including battered fingers.' He reached for the bandaged hand and moved strong fingers around her wrist.

'Wha—what are you doing?' she asked, suddenly afraid of the latent power in his hand. She looked down at it, seeing the way the dark hairs curled over its back. He was very masculine and she could not help remembering the times those hands had been run through her hair, bringing her almost to a state of collapse as he had pulled her taut against his body. She trembled and the fingers tightened.

'Please!' she whispered. 'You're hurting me.'

At once he relaxed his hold, and let her hand rest gently back on the blanket.

'You're almost over the shock,' he told her. 'Your hand isn't trembling as much as when I came in.'

She glanced down at her hand, realising the truth of his words.

'Then there's nothing more to keep you here, is there?' she demanded, acid sweet.

'My word, we are petty, aren't we?' he chuckled, thrusting both hands deep in trouser pockets below his open mess jacket. 'You know what we do with spoiled children who've hurt themselves and come crying to Mummy?'

'Oh, shut up and go away!'

'When I'm ready.' The hands came out of the pockets and rested hard upon her shoulders, pushing her against the couch's back. 'We *kiss* the pain better. Like this.' His mouth was on hers, warm and firm. She was so startled that she was unable to resist. He moved back a little, probing her eyes with his. 'And perhaps even more so . . .' His left hand slid from her shoulder to her neck, first finger and thumb gripping her chin, while his mouth crushed hers. She wriggled beneath him. The cup and saucer fell with a clatter to the floor and her good hand came up to catch him a severe blow on the neck. He jerked back, gasping. Her hand had been a closed fist. For a frightening moment she thought he might kill her. His dark face was black with fury and ripples of fire sparkled in his eyes. He stood erect, holding her gaze.

'My God!' he whispered. 'I pity the man who eventually wins you. The poor sap will lead a dog's life. Heaven be praised I learned the truth before it was too late!'

He spun on his heel and left her. Fiona leaned forward, sobbing bitterly. A moment later, Robert and Sandra were in the doorway, staring in horror.

'Whatever's the matter?' Robert asked.

'I . . . I dropped the cup and it smashed. I'm so sorry.' Fiona wailed in reply. Sandra stooped to retrieve the pieces, but her eyes sought Robert's and a message flashed between them. Had Fiona been able to see it, she might have read it as saying:

'It's more than the cup which has broken.'

CHAPTER FOUR

IN spite of the drug prescribed for her, Fiona spent an almost sleepless night; a night filled with disturbing dreams. She was with Alan, who mocked and chided her; Alan who bent over her, kissing her again and again until she cried out with the pain of bruised lips; an Alan after whom she was running, but could never quite reach ...

She was thankful to see the dawn peep through the curtained window and lay awake, waiting for the early morning tea to arrive.

The majority of the passengers arose early, eager for their first glimpse of Lisbon and the day ashore, but Fiona was unable to summon any interest. Her hand was terribly sore, her head ached and the thought of food nauseated her until Sandra persuaded her to eat at least one of the hot, crisp rolls that had been brought for breakfast and to drink a strong cup of coffee. She then felt a little better.

'You ought to rest in bed until later,' Sandra advised. 'I'll keep very quiet and not disturb you.'

'But you were going ashore with Peter and Julia!' Fiona protested.

'No. I'd rather stay with you.'

Fiona propped herself on her good elbow.

'I'd hate you to spoil your day on my account. Please, Sandra, go with them. I shouldn't feel right knowing I'd kept you with me. Besides,' she forced a wry smile, 'about an hour of my grouchy company will finish you! No, much as I enjoy having you with me, I'd much prefer to be on my own all day and do just what I feel like doing. So off you go and have a good time.'

'Are you sure? I mean, I feel awfully guilty about leaving you with your bad hand.'

'You can't take it with you!' Fiona laughed. 'Make the most of the time ashore.'

'You're very generous ...'

'No, just selfish. If you're not here, I won't feel I have to make conversation. I can do exactly as I like; snooze, read, walk the deck, anything. If you stayed, you'd be bored to tears and just as bad-tempered as me by dinner tonight! I shall look forward to hearing all about it when you get back.'

Before they left the liner, Peter and Julia called to find out how Fiona was feeling. They told her how sorry they were she felt unwell and parted with the promise to bring her back a nice surprise.

Fiona expected to go down to the hospital but, to her surprise, shortly after the other three had left for disembarkation, there came a knock at the cabin door. Robert entered and Fiona rose from the bed on which she had been sitting, placing small items she thought she might need inside a handbag.

'Hallo,' she said, 'I was just about to come and pay you a visit.' He settled himself beside her, reaching for the sling.

'Well? How is it?'

'Oh, all right, I suppose.'

'Bad night?'

'Terrible, actually.' She grinned at him. 'As for those beastly drugs you gave me, I don't want any more. When I wasn't awake, I dozed off into the most awful nightmares.'

'I was afraid they might have that effect. Better now?'

She sighed.

'I've one thumper of a head, but the coffee I drank at breakfast seems to be of some help. Sandra almost forced it down my throat.'

'I met her just before she and your other two friends went ashore. I thought perhaps you wouldn't really be up to gallivanting on dry land today. It's a pity. Still, we'll make it up to you later. I'd like to re-dress the knuckles. I'll be in the hospital until about noon, so just drop in whenever you feel like it. By the way, I have an old friend living in Madeira, and she'd love you and Sandra to visit with me. Will you come? Don't you dare say no, because Sandra's been approached already. I'm relying on you, my dear, to make up her mind for her!' His eyes twinkled mischievously at her.

'I see. I'm to play gooseberry, is that it?'

'Observant little soul, aren't you? I suppose you might say your surmise is correct. I know one thing, however; if you refuse, she won't accept either, especially after this. She blurted out to me just now about going off and leaving you—guilt and suchlike.'

'I'd prefer to have the day to myself, then I can moan and groan to my heart's content,' said Fiona.

'I gave her my professional opinion, which was almost along the same lines as you. Couched in politer terms, naturally. So Sandra therefore feels she can't neglect you in future. Where you go, she'll go, and vice versa. I want her to visit my friend with me ...'

'And I have to be asked as well?' Fiona was not annoyed at the blatant obviousness of Robert's invitation. The thought struck her blindingly that had Alan been in his place, she would have flown into a rage and taken him violently to task. Not for Alan Howard would she have played gooseberry, prickly or otherwise!

'You have a soft spot for my friend, perhaps?' she probed gently.

'Right on target. I may be a crusty bachelor, but never in my life have I been so overwhelmed by one particular woman. I must admit, when first I set eyes on her, I was totally unprepared for the ferocity of the complaint under which I now labour.' He tapped his chest in the region of his heart and gave a wry smile. 'Bad palpitations. Only one cure, I'm afraid, and I want you to help me. If you will, of course.' He shifted his position so that he was more comfortable, leaning back to rest his head against the bulkhead. 'I want to know all about her. I've time to spare for a quick chat before returning to my somewhat arduous morning duties. To boot, one hand has to be re-dressed!'

Fiona began to relate everything she knew about Sandra, which was not very much, and which certainly did not satisfy the eager young man at her side. Every now and again he interposed a question. They had been in conversation for about five minutes when there came a firm knock on the door. Neither moved from the bed as Fiona called out:

'Come in!'

She did not realise the cosy picture of intimacy which she and Robert presented to Alan as he came into the cabin. Robert did, and moved closer to Fiona, a wicked twinkle in his eye. Alan scowled.

'I came to enquire how you were. I noticed you didn't go ashore with your friends. Doctor Maynard, what are you doing here?' He snapped the question.

'Taking her pulse, of course,' came the rather mocking reply. Robert stood up and pulled down the back of his jacket which had become creased. 'I'll see you in about half an hour's time, perhaps?' he asked Fiona, who nodded.

'Don't let me send you away when it's only too obvious you have a great deal to say to each other!' Alan sneered unpleasantly. Robert's eyelids flickered. 'I would have waited for you to come on deck, but there's something I thought you might be interested to see, Miss Barclay.'

'Oh?' The question was offhand.

'The *Sagres* is setting sail to our starboard. She's a beautiful sight. You recall, perhaps, my mentioning the Sail Training Association's *Malcolm Miller* a few years back?' Alan appeared to have forgotten the doctor's presence and that astute young officer certainly did not follow up with a remark about not realising his superior had been acquainted with his patient before the start of the cruise. Instead he slipped from the cabin.

'The *Sagres*? Oh yes, I'd love to see her,' was Fiona's eager response. Alan reached down a hand to slide beneath her elbow, helping her to her feet. He followed her into the passage and together they went on deck. There were few other passengers about, most of them having gone ashore. The big white square-rigger was passing slowly to starboard, her heavy sails falling open to the wind as the yards were swung round. Blocks squealed and boys worked with obvious eagerness. The magnificent red cross which decorated each sail caught the sun's rays as it bellied and became firm in the gentle wind. With Alan close at her side, Fiona watched breathlessly. There was something about the beautiful ship which caught and tugged at her heartstrings.

'Like all schoolships, she's manned mainly by youngsters,' Alan told her. 'It's a tough school. Those great crosses on the sails still proclaim the scarlet Cross of Christ.'

'How do they know what to do and which rope to use?'

Fiona asked in bewilderment at the mass of running rigging on the ship. There were so many sheets and halliards that to the uninitiated they looked like a gigantic confusion of rope. 'I could never do their job. I simply wouldn't know which was what.'

'It's a skill to be learned with patience and great perseverance.'

'And standing up there on those thin ropes beneath the big yards!' she shuddered. 'I'd be dizzy before I'd climbed ten yards above the deck.' Her gaze had caught the group of young boys now treading the foot ropes, their bodies supported by the yards. 'Have you ever sailed on a boat like this?'

'Ship, my love, not boat. No, I haven't, but I wish I'd had the opportunity. By crewing on a ship like the *Sagres* a man learns the true meaning of seamanship, an art which can't really be learned from working aboard a motor vessel. Navigation, yes, but not sailing. To use the might of the wind to the best advantage, that's the beauty of such lovely ships. I've done dinghy sailing which is exciting and exhilarating, but nothing compared to the great teamwork needed for working a square-rigger. Perhaps you know the origin of her name?' He looked down at her and saw the shake of her head. 'She's named after the flat headland from which Prince Henry the Navigator watched his ships set sail for the very ends of the world. An apt and fine name, don't you think?'

The big vessel was drawing away very swiftly, her clean white bow slicing majestically through brilliant blue water, dividing it into curls of foam. Fiona could not tear away her eyes; the ship seemed to mesmerise her. She felt a great wave of sadness and was alarmed when tears blurred her vision. She must not let Alan see her cry! she thought in panic, turning her head slightly so that he could no longer watch her profile. But why the tears? Grief for all that the *Sagres* signified? The eras gone by. The years which might have been spent with this man at her side? For stupidity and childish fears. And now *Sagres* was moving away, just as Alan's love for her had vanished. *Sagres* epitomised the past; she was a reminder of the days when men had to be fearfully tough and resilient to survive the harsh rigours of a life at sea as they traded throughout the world. It was a strange and frightening sensation, to stand here and watch this graceful memory of the past slide into the distance, while with it went the ghost of a life which could have been hers, had she acted differently.

And what did Alan think of her now? He had not wanted any explanation of her conduct, yet what had been his feelings on learning she had run from him? If only she could explain! If only he would warm towards her a little so that she might find the courage to raise the matter with him. But why was there this urgent need to do so? Her own guilt? The weight of her own conscience which was becoming unbearable? Was it not just a selfish desire to shift her almost intolerable burden on to other shoulders, regardless of the pain of the past which might be evoked in the heart of the listener? Yes, that was it. She felt guilty at having treated him so badly. Guilt was a beastly feeling to live with. Well, she was stuck with it now, so she must make the best of a bad job. On no account must she give in to the temptation of pouring her reasons into Alan's totally unsympathetic ear. Not now. Not ever. Because he no longer liked her.

She turned her head slightly and realised that he had been studying her. Colour began to tinge her cheeks.

'Thank you for coming to fetch me to see the *Sagres*,'

she said in a rigidly controlled voice. 'If you hadn't, then I might not have known until later, when I'd have missed a wonderful sight.'

He moved so that his back was against the deck rail. Idly he crossed one leg over the other and she noticed the well-polished shoes. With no regard for the shape of his garment, he thrust both hands into trouser pockets and let out a long sigh. Her eyebrows quirked. He smiled at her.

'Sorry,' he said. 'Just thinking, that's all.'

'I suppose it's a great and heavy responsibility being the captain of a cruise liner as big as this?'

'It has its attendant problems, agreed, and some more arduous than others.' He lifted his left arm to study his wrist-watch. 'Ah well, can't idle here all morning. Look after that hand, won't you?'

Fiona followed him with her eyes as he strode away, his tall, lean figure erect as his long legs covered the deck. When he had gone, it seemed to her that the sun had gone behind a cloud. She remained at the rail for another minute, then turned to go to the lounge, which was empty. A steward brought piping hot coffee, which was delicious. She drank two cups and nibbled a sweet biscuit. After she had finished she went to the sick bay for her hand to be dressed.

'Aching a bit?' Robert asked as he gently unwound the bandage. She admitted that it was rather painful. He bent over the badly bruised fingers and felt along the length of each. 'You've been lucky. Those doors are very heavy. A dry dressing, I think, except here, where the skin is broken.' He opened a tube of soothing ointment and spread a generous amount over the torn area. Fiona said nothing while he re-bandaged the hand. When he had finished he straightened, gave her a studied look, and then announced:

'I'm on my way to the infants' play area. Coming?'

'Have you many little ones on board?'

'About twelve.' He grinned at her. 'I'll let you into a little secret. No matter how busy I am here, I try to steal the odd quarter of an hour to spend with the toddlers.' He touched his chest. 'Soft spot of mine, kids.'

'You'd like a family of your own?'

'Very much.' He cleared his throat. 'And I don't mind telling you that I think it's possible I might be getting nearer to my goal. 'Nuff said! Come on!'

The play area was on the promenade deck, just above the sick bay, so they had a short flight of stairs to negotiate. Fiona heard the happy laughter long before they entered the play deck. A young girl in a short white dress and tiny cap was perched on the edge of a sandpit, watching a tiny blonde child of about three industriously fill her bucket; while, a short distance from them both, a boy of four began to empty out his own bucket, then rubbed the falling sand with his bare feet.

'Good morning, Miss Sharp. Everything all right?' Robert asked.

'Yes, thank you, sir.'

'This is Miss Barclay. She had a slight contretemps with a door last night.'

'I hope you're feeling better now?' the girl asked, and Fiona nodded.

'Thanks to the good doctor.'

There was a burst of childish laughter from the playroom adjoining the sandpit and they all turned their heads. Robert tucked his arm through Fiona's.

'Let's go and see what's going on.'

The room was large and airy, with brightly coloured

decorations to catch a youngster's eye. Another children's supervisor was kneeling on the floor helping a chubby baby fit together the pieces of a wooden engine and tender while, to Fiona's intense surprise and disbelief, Alan sat on a low chair, a tiny girl cradled in his arms. In the corner of the room, three other children were absorbed in play with dolls and toys. Alan bent his head and said something to the little girl. She turned wide blue eyes to Fiona and Robert, then stuck her thumb in her mouth.

'I see you've found an admirer, Alan,' Robert chuckled.

'It appears so. This is Amanda. She's rather shy, I'm afraid, so I ...' Alan faltered slightly, '... I ... Miss Hudson is otherwise engaged with the trials and tribulations of the railways.' Fiona saw his left arm ease the child on his knee closer. Soft hair touched his jacket and the big blue eyes began to close. There was an expression of deep tenderness on his face as he studied his charge. In a soft tone he remarked: 'I think it's time for a short nap, Miss Hudson, when you're free.'

The supervisor glanced up, smiled in a friendly fashion and replied:

'I'll relieve you of her in a moment, sir.'

Fiona took a step forward, then faltered, a blush rising to her cheek. It had been a natural reaction to want to blurt out that she would hold the baby until the other girl was free, but she had forgotten her slinged arm. She was deeply conscious of Alan's thoughtful gaze upon her; a gaze she dared not meet lest he read her inner turmoil.

This was a side of him she had not seen! Before their planned marriage, they had discussed having children once or twice, Fiona presuming that a family would arrive eventually because that was part of nature, but there had been no mention of any intense yearning for a child by either of them. It had been a subject which was almost semi-taboo. How little she had known him! she decided. She had refused to probe beneath the surface; refused to look further and learn what manner of man he was.

Now the children's supervisor was lifting the child from Alan's arms, cradling her against her body in such a way that she would not waken. Alan stretched his legs and rose from the chair with a fluid yet languid movement which put Fiona in mind of a sleepy cat on a hot summer's afternoon. He had a few quiet words with the girl, nodded to Robert and Fiona, and left the playroom. As he passed one of the children who was playing on the floor, he patted the curly head and was swiftly rewarded by a flow of quite unintelligible chatter. He laughed.

Fiona remained with Robert in the playroom for a further ten minutes, but the children were rather shy of her and afraid to come too close because of the sling around her arm.

'What are your plans for the rest of the day?' Robert asked when finally they left the children's area.

'I thought of finding a nice sunny place, a good book, a comfy cushion, and have a good sleep.'

'Then watch the sun and don't overdo it the first time. I don't want you sick with heat-stroke or something like that.' He glanced at his watch. Fiona smiled.

'There's still a great many hours until they return,' she teased. Robert pinched her arm in retaliation.

'I could give as good as I get, you know. For instance,' he declared, not looking at her, 'Alan was once engaged, only it was broken off right at the last minute. It hit him hard and ...'

'Have you known him long?' she interrupted quickly.

'Yes. About ten years, give and take a few years between

when we didn't see each other because he was in dock when I was at the far ends of the earth, and vice versa. He'd asked me to be best man at his wedding, but I had to decline, being thousands of miles away at the time. Doesn't talk about it now, of course, but he's altered considerably during the past three or more years. Being a medic, I tried to persuade him to talk about it, to get it out of his system, but he wouldn't.' He dipped into his pocket and pulled out a packet of cigarettes, offering one to Fiona, who declined.

'I don't, thank you.'

'Mind if I do?'

'Please go ahead.'

He lit up slowly, exhaling a long stream of smoke before continuing:

'I'm not exactly blind, Fiona. I believe you're still in love with him. What went wrong? Like to tell me so that I can help you both?'

She was astounded and gasped:

'Is . . . is it so obvious? About . . .'

'Your feelings for Alan? Not obvious, no, but I have an extra pair of eyes . . . X-ray eyes. Did you talk to anyone after you jilted him?' She winced at his choice of word. 'He's a good man, Fiona. I think you're both ideally suited, but if there's this great barrier between you, then someone ought to step in and help crumble it.'

Fiona sighed.

'Oh, Robert, what's the use? He doesn't like me now. What I did . . . jilting him, if you like . . . killed any love he had for me. No one can revive a cold, dead fire.'

He flicked ash from his cigarette.

'If it were possible, would you want it?' he asked slowly. 'Do you want to turn back the clock to where it was before you . . . er . . . split up?'

She considered the question before making any reply. To return to those days just before the wedding date? Oh no! It must never be like that again. It was the truth she spoke.

'No, Robert, I never want that kind of time again. I've accepted my lot. Or, if you like, I've made my bed and must lie on it.'

'Alone, of course?'

'Alone, naturally.'

'Ah, well, I've done my best. As long as this cruise isn't proving too burdensome for you, being in love with Alan, yet knowing there's no future.'

'I've faced up to the facts, and I can manage, I assure you.' She found his hand and squeezed it. 'But thank you for trying. Alan and I can take care of ourselves. Oh, you won't tell him about this conversation, will you?'

'Of course not! It wouldn't be ethical. After all, you're one of my patients.'

Sandra returned to the ship after her trip to Lisbon full of gay chatter at all she had seen and done ashore. Throughout dinner that evening, when they were under way again and Lisbon falling quickly astern, the passengers seemed to have one topic of conversation only ... Lisbon and its beauties.

Two days later Fiona joined a small party to go ashore at Lanzarote, where she experienced an interesting yet rather queasy camel ride up the slopes of Mount Mirado to look at the breathtaking view from its summit. She wanted to stay there and stare and stare. The air was so clear, the colours sharp and bright, the outlines finely etched, and the air itself a luxury of balmy warmth. After the camel ride, where Fiona had to hang on tightly for fear she might slide off the heaving back, they visited the sixteenth-century castles of San Gabriel and San José and the Church of San Gines. Because her hand was not yet fully healed, Fiona skipped a swim in the crystal waters of El Golfo lagoon, sitting at its edge beside Sandra, both of them dangling bare legs in the water. Sandra studied the emerald green water and sighed with envy.

'I could have taken a dip today, I suppose, but Robert advised me to wait a few more days. He said it was too soon after my operation, and he was afraid I might get cramp. Cramp! In these warm waters?'

Fiona chuckled.

'I expect what he really meant was that he would rather keep an eye on you in the ship's pool when you take your first swim. In case of cramp, naturally,' she finished with a broad grin. Sandra nudged her.

'I know *exactly* what you mean!' she retorted.

'Well, he did ask you to have three dances last night. And he seems to spend a great deal of his time perambulating about the deck whenever he might possibly hope to find you snoring in a deck chair. I sometimes wonder what you'd both do if there were an outbreak of bubonic plague, or something as frightful, aboard. No coffee, no tea and biscuits, no dancing, no knee-nudging under the table at dinner and ...'

'I *don't* nudge his knee!'

'Oh? Then who thought it was you last night and kept on poking me hard?'

'You've just made that up! Beast!'

They both laughed, then Fiona asked gently:

'You do like him, don't you, Sandra?'

'Yes, I do.'

Fiona touched her hand.

'I'm so glad. I think he's . . . how can I describe him except by saying he's a perfect love. How's that? I see you approve. But you're not to worry, because I haven't set my sights on him. You have the field to yourself. Except for the new rival . . . Mrs Bottlin-Mabee!' she teased.

'Don't!' Sandra moaned feelingly. 'That woman! Poor, poor Robert!'

'I wonder what happened to alienate her and the captain? She was chasing him wholeheartedly a couple of days ago.'

'Robert told me.' Sandra began to laugh. 'I meant to tell you yesterday, but it slipped my mind. Only don't for goodness' sake breathe a word to anyone else, otherwise Robert will be in dire trouble with his captain.'

'Do go on! I'm intrigued.' Fiona wrapped her arms about her knees.

'As you know, the officer and crew's quarters are out of bounds to all passengers, unless they're summoned to the captain's august presence. Well, the other night Mrs Bottlin-Mabee managed to attach herself to the captain, forcing him to dance twice with her, as no doubt you noticed. Unfortunately this triumph drove her to the bottle and she became quite tiddly with success. She clung like a limpet until he inveigled someone to send for him to the bridge; thence he made his escape and remained there until about two in the morning. At such a time all late-night revellers should be sound asleep in their beds, Mrs B-M included. He went to his cabin where, to his horror, he found that good lady curled up asleep on his bunk. How she got there was a mystery until the following morning when the furious captain learned she'd bribed one of the stewards with a large sum of money to let her into the cabin. The steward concerned is being disciplined, so Robert says.'

'Poor man! I'm sure there are mitigating circumstances. That woman is totally overbearing, as Alan well knows!'

'Three of them had to cart her off to bed and there she stayed all the next day, moaning about a terrible germ she must have picked up in Lisbon because her head ached so badly! Robert gave her the standard treatment for a hangover, but as far as she's concerned, she believes he saved her from a deadly foreign virus. Hence the resultant attachment. And the captain has avoided her ever since. She hasn't tried to seek him out, so no doubt her memory serves her pretty well, imaginary virus or no!'

'We shall have to join forces to prevent her from bulldozing Robert. All the same, I can't help feeling sorry for the florid middle-aged ladies who labour under the delusion that they're God's gift to man, however old they are.' Fiona finished with a touch of genuine sympathy, 'Unfortunately, some of them are not merely pathetic, when you feel you can excuse their behaviour, but downright aggressive as well. This is what I find so terribly embarrassing about it. I often wonder if, when my time comes, and I perhaps have a tendency towards this kind of thing, will I notice and be able to stop myself in time?'

Sandra laughed loudly, her voice bell-like. '*You?*' she echoed in plain disbelief. 'Heavens, no! The types that turn out to be Bottlin-Mabees are those dreadful women who've married money and mouselike husbands who, poor dears, seek early refuge in death, leaving their wives with golden handshakes to do with as they please. And off they go, preying like sharks upon the ocean deeps. Cruises are always their favourite targets, especially when the captains happen to be as young and as good-looking as your Alan Howard. Also, and here's the rub, even more enticing are they if they're unmarried. Which reminds me, Fiona, are you managing all right?'

'How do you mean?'

'With our captain. Being old friends and breaking it up. Don't you now wish that things had turned out a little differently?' Fiona refused to look at her friend, tracing instead the striations of rock beside her with her forefinger. 'Robert likes him a great deal, you know. They're good friends. Oh, he hasn't betrayed any secrets, I promise. No, Robert can be clamlike when he wants to, but I know he would like Alan to be happier than he is at the moment.' Fiona's eyelids flickered. 'For your information, my dear, Alan Howard is an extremely unhappy man. We can almost feel the awkward atmosphere between the two of you, in spite of the exquisite politeness you each show in public.' Sandra sighed and stretched her body languidly, closing her eyes to stare up at the sun. 'Do you know what I think you should do? Apologise for whatever it was you said to him when you had your last furious row.'

'But we didn't have one!' Fiona exploded with considerable anger. 'It was nothing like that. It was a mutual agreement to part. At least ...' her white teeth sank into the edge of her lower lip and a tear sparkled on her eyelashes. 'That's not true. There was no row, because I funked it. I ran away. I left Alan to find out from my father that I didn't want to marry him, and until we came aboard last week I hadn't seen him since that day.'

Sandra let out a long-drawn sigh.

'Oh, Fiona!' she whispered sadly. 'Just think how hurt he must have been! But you're speaking now. Don't you think ... I mean, couldn't you tell him how sorry you are that you behaved in that manner? It might help, even though it was so long ago. My parents always taught me that where apologies are concerned, there can never be a time-limit; although, of course, it's preferable to make them as soon as you become aware that you've offended someone.' She caught Fiona's sun-drenched wrist, feeling the warmth beneath her fingers and a slight tremor which she put down to emotion. 'It's hateful having to say you're sorry, but afterwards you begin to feel so much better. Ask to see the captain! I'm sure he'd find time. Will you?'

Fiona was undecided. Had not Alan said that he no longer cared about the past? That it was over and done with and he needed no reminders? Why had he told her this? To save her the necessity of feeling that she *ought* to give him some kind of explanation? But this would be no explanation, but an apology, and neither of them had said a word about apologies. It was true she felt desperately guilty and ought not to unload that guilt on Alan. But she had been wrong to treat him as she had done. He must surely feel bitter because she had left her father to do the explaining for her. After all, she wasn't exactly asking him to take her back, or to say she wished she hadn't behaved in such a stupid manner! No, all she wanted to do was to apologise for that stupidity. She could not tell him now how much she regretted her action; that she had come to realise how much she loved him still. He would accuse her of trying to throw herself at him. A second Mrs Bottlin-Mabee! Heavens, no! Just the apology. Simple, short but sincere . . .

Aloud she replied:

'If you really think I should speak to him, then I will.' Sandra leaned across to kiss her.

'And if I've judged the captain aright, he'll accept your apology and you can both start to rebuild from there.'

Fiona chose not to delude her. Instinctively she knew that Alan would offer no reasons for the rebuilding of their relationship. But at least, metaphorically speaking, she could draw a firm, clear line beneath that particular chapter and close the book for good.

The liner was under way again, this time bound for Tenerife, which island they were due to reach early the following morning. It was to be a short stay of eight hours only, and both girls had planned to go ashore to see as much of the island as possible.

The liner was very gay that evening. On deck a horse-race was in progress, with crowds of passengers gathered beneath the coloured lights, watching the competitors vie with each other. For the more elderly, a bingo session was busily under way in one of the smaller lounges, while the boisterous laughter and music of a cabaret could be heard issuing in gusts from the main lounge every time some-one opened a door.

After trying their hands ... very unsuccessfully ... at horse-racing, Sandra and Fiona were joined by Robert, who told them brightly that he had abandoned his two patients in the sick bay for the night. He attached himself to Sandra and escorted both girls to the bar where they made themselves comfortable with long drinks.

'Any dire disease below?' Fiona teased, and Robert shook his curly head.

'Nothing that time won't heal. But my lips are sealed. Whatever ails my patients is a closely guarded secret, save to say that I believe them both to be well on the way to total recovery. Fiona, your attention is wandering. For whom are you looking, or need I ask?'

Fiona coloured quickly, her skin almost matching the soft rose of her sleeveless tricel dress.

'I ...' she began, when Sandra explained for her.

'We're waiting for a message, that's all.'

'Indeed?' Robert breathed excitedly. 'Do I detect skulduggery? Care to let a fellow in on a secret?'

'Certainly not!' Sandra retorted with a wink at the other girl. 'You may have your Hippocratic oath while we have our own code. This is nice,' she sipped appreciatively at the drink. 'What is it?'

'Pimms, with a mixture of something else added. Special Maynard Brew, guaranteed to put a sparkle into your eyes and a lilt to your heart.'

A white-coated steward was approaching with a silver tray. He paused to ask:

'Miss Barclay?'

'Yes.'

'A message for you, miss.' He proffered the tray under Fiona's nose. With a slightly shaking hand she picked up the sealed white envelope.

'Thank you.'

Sandra said nothing, watching as Fiona slit the envelope and extracted the doubled paper.

'Will you excuse me, please?' Fiona asked a trifle breathlessly as she stood up. 'I hope I won't be long.'

They had been waiting all evening for this response to the letter she had written after returning to the ship. It had not been an easy note to pen, because she had not wanted to make it sound too friendly or presuming. Finally Sandra had dictated the brief missive; a polite request to see Alan on a matter of importance. He had not been at dinner, so Fiona had been obliged to curb her impatience until now. As so often happens in such circumstances, once the summons arrives, the urge for it dies abruptly. She wished with all her heart that she had ignored Sandra's advice and left well alone. For some reason, she felt nothing good would come of resurrecting the past like this, but it was done.

She had to go through with it. Far better to face whatever was coming and finish with it. Alan's reply stated tersely that he would see her in his cabin at her earliest convenience.

Fiona went to the purser's office where she explained to his deputy that the captain wished to see her and could she please be escorted? Within minutes a white-coated steward was walking ahead of her along the corridors which led to the officers' quarters. She thought she might have been able to remember the way alone, but with the tale of Mrs Bottlin-Mabee in mind, she decided to take the wiser course of being shown to the cabin.

The steward knocked on the door, announced her arrival, and then withdrew, closing the door behind him. Fiona felt as if she stood in a strong wind and clasped her hands tightly together while Alan's keen and unfriendly eyes appraised hers. After a faulty start, she managed to say:

'It was kind of you to agree to seeing me.'

'Not at all. It's my duty to see that my passengers have everything they require. Is something amiss with your accommodation, or have you a complaint to register?' He was dressed in a casual shirt and well-tailored linen slacks. On Fiona's arrival, he had been standing at his desk with a book in his hand. She had watched him lay this down, spine upwards, and then turn slowly towards her, both hands moving in a languid fashion to the side pockets of his slacks. He was leaning against the desk now, and she saw the faint movement of one thumb within the pocket.

'No, I . . . I have no complaint,' she replied.

'I see. Will you sit down?'

'Thank you. It would be easier.' She waited while he indicated a comfortable armchair, then settled herself, carefully folding her skirt over her knees and conscious of his gaze travelling from there to her trim ankles and back. Apart from indicating the chair, he had not moved. He looked so relaxed that she envied him greatly. Her stomach was curled into a tight little ball and the palms of her hands had become embarrassingly sticky. She would have liked to take out her handkerchief and wipe them on it, but she dared not, lest he see her discomfort.

'Well, what is it?' he asked, his voice impatient.

'You're not making it very easy for me ...'

'Why should I when I haven't the least notion what's bothering you?'

'I wanted to ... Alan, I felt I should apologise. Oh, I know it's coming far too late to do any good, but it's been worrying me for some time. I'm not asking you to forgive and forget, because I know that's pretty impossible. No, all I want to say is that I really am truly and deeply sorry for treating you as I did three years ago.' Her head was bent. She sensed rather than saw him ease his hands from the pockets, straighten his back and then wander across to the shelf on which stood a tray and decanter, plus clean glasses. There was a long silence, broken only by the scrape of the decanter knob, the splash of liquid into a glass, and then he was beside her, the glass extended to her. She shook her head.

'Then you don't mind if I do?' he asked, lifting the glass to his lips. When he had drunk half of the contents, he continued:

'If I may be so bold, why have you decided now, after all this time, that an apology is due?'

'I'm not sure. It's just that ... well, seeing you again, and having the past brought back so vividly ... I did you a grave injustice, and an apology, however inane it could sound, should be given.'

'I see.' The voice was hard and there was a tinkle as he set the glass back on the silver tray. He returned to the desk, both hands behind him to grip its edge, and then addressed her.

'You expect me to believe this?'

Her head shot up.

'Why not?'

'For one simple reason! It reeks of falsehood.'

Angered, she leapt up.

'That isn't true! I meant what I said, whether you care to believe me or not. I really am very sorry I behaved as I did. I suppose I must have had my reasons . . .'

He did not allow her to complete the sentence.

'As you have them for coming here this evening. Oh, my dear, I can read you like this book!' He picked up the open book and flapped its pages before her. 'I know why you came running here to see me. You're thinking that you missed out badly three years ago. That you threw away an excellent opportunity and that if you play your cards right, I'll be willing to take you back on the same terms as before. But you're wrong, my sweet. Terribly, terribly wrong!' She began to expostulate, but he silenced her with one hand. 'It must have been a ghastly shock to find that I was the captain of this vessel. You never thought I'd progress so far, did you? You presumed I'd be stuck to the old rusting banana-type tub, with few prospects of promotion, and somehow that didn't suit your book, did it, miss? Oh no! But now everything's very different. To be the wife of the captain of a large cruise ship—how proud and grand it will make you before your friends! However, you've miscalculated. I don't want you, my dear.'

Fire burned in Fiona's cheeks and there was a furious sparkle in her eyes. She glared at him, reached out to snatch the book from him and tossed it so hard on to the desk that it overshot and fell on to the floor beyond.

'Such thoughts never entered my head!' she snapped back. 'I came here because I thought you'd understand. What I did to you was despicable. I should have stayed to speak to you myself. Instead I left it to my unfortunate father who, bless his soul, agreed against his wish to tell you I no longer wanted to marry you.'

'Ah, yes, your decision! Now that the subject is in the open, do you consider you could possibly bring yourself to tell me your reasons for the abrupt reversal of intent?' he enquired, his voice low and full of menace. 'But first, perhaps, I ought to tell you how your father explained the position to me. I arrived back in the country, eager to be with you, and eager for our wedding day. Your letter said you couldn't come to the dock, or see me again. Therefore I went straight to your house, only to learn that you'd run away. Run away!' His laugh was mockingly unpleasant. 'Run away from me, who was to be your loving husband. And after those sweet, gentle letters you'd written me! I think I can be forgiven for not believing your father at first. I asked to see you, but you were nowhere to be found. Just a message left for me. "Please tell Alan that I don't love him, so I'm not going to marry him on Saturday." As simple as that. Only I didn't think it *was* so simple. I'm afraid I gave your father an uncomfortable time with my demands for the truth and my badgering questions. All he could say was to repeat your message ... Fiona doesn't love you and thinks it would be a grave mistake for both of you to go through with it ... Then I asked where I might find you, but once again I drew a blank. Your father knew where you'd gone, but apparently I was not to be told. I was not even allowed to seek you out for myself, to talk to you, to discover for myself what troubled you and to try and talk you round. You see, Fiona, I loved you very deeply at that time, and I was almost demented with pain . . .'

'I'm sorry, Alan,' she whispered, her heart blistering from the harshness of his tone. 'I did wrong. I should have told you and not left it to Dad.'

'I agree. It would have been good manners to see me in person. However, you didn't. I tried all kinds of ways of finding you, but each time I drew a blank. I returned to the ship a completely different man . . . bitter and tormented. And, my sweet, I vowed then and there that I'd never allow another woman to break down my defences.' He reached out a hand and caught one of hers, jerking her to an upright position. 'Look at me, Fiona! Take a good, long look. Once you held my heart in the palm of this hand. Now no one owns it and no one ever will.' His tight lip curled into an unpleasant sneer. 'How I've lived since that time three years ago can be of no interest to you, but I shan't admit to being entirely celibate. I'm a man. I have the natural instincts and cravings of a normal man of my years, but not once has my heart been involved. So you can put away any ideas rushing about that cunning head of yours that I might want you back, because I don't. Not under those same terms.'

'I've already said I'm sorry.'

'So you have. It must be quite a disappointment to you,' he continued, his tone bitingly sarcastic. 'I'm sorry if I've destroyed any fine-flung dreams you might have been nourishing these past few days about the two of us resuming our engagement where it was so untidily broken off.'

'No, Alan, that wasn't my intention.'

'Then why did you come here? Why didn't you leave

well alone if there wasn't some further purpose in your mind?' She bit her lip. 'Of course it could be that you've been feeling guilty about the past. Seeing me once more merely revived the guilt and it's become such a heavy burden that you hoped to shift it most conveniently on to my shoulders instead, so that you could go ahead and have a good time on your own.'

'How dare you!' she snapped, angry that he should have touched so neatly on part of the truth. But her mission was failing. If anything, her guilt had been intensified by this discussion. She must leave him at once, before she broke down and cried in front of him. She made a blundering movement towards the door, but he reached out and caught her, jerking her roughly back to face him.

'Not so fast, my dear! *You* may have finished, but I haven't. Since you've brought the matter into the open after lying uneasily for three years, let us pursue it further.' His fingers moved to her chin, gripping her so hard that she was obliged to stare up into eyes which gleamed like twin coals. She felt afraid of his magnetism and began to tremble, a fact he noted with some satisfaction.

'Are you still afraid of me? You know, I did an enormous amount of thinking after that unhappy leave. I wondered what it was that had driven you to fall out of love with me. I came to all kinds of conclusion, yet none satisfied me in the least. However, after a few weeks, it gradually dawned on me that perhaps I'd been partly to blame. I concluded that you no longer loved me because I hadn't sufficiently demonstrated my own love for you. I'd treated you like the inexperienced child you so obviously were. Instead of wooing you, teaching you what love is, I was afraid to touch you as a man should touch the woman he's about to marry. My kisses were too gentle, hands still instead of caressing

... go ahead and blush, it's very becoming ... I should have been more positive in my approach to you, bringing you almost to the point of surrender so that you longed impatiently for the day when my gold band was on your finger. But I failed you. I walked off that ship, anxious for our wedding night when the mysteries would be explained to you in my actions, but my pretty little bird had flown. Do you understand the meaning of the word "torment"? I doubt it. But that's all water under the bridge now. Since then I expect you've had many men wooing and winning you, although you're still unmarried. Is there a man in the offing?'

'How delicately you phrase your questions!' she retaliated.

'So there's no one. Pity. He might have made up for my lapse.' He released her and turned away, clearing his throat before he dropped his bomb-shell. 'We've discussed the past. Let's now turn to the future. I don't want to marry you, Fiona. However, that wish certainly doesn't preclude any other thoughts I might have concerning you. During these intervening years you've become very beautiful and intensely desirable—yes, jerk those eyebrows at me in disbelief; it's true. As I've already admitted, I'm a man, with normal instincts. Do you understand me?'

Her heart was pounding within her. Whatever was he driving at? Where was all this leading? If only she could reach the door and escape his intensely personal interrogation!

He moved towards her.

'I wonder ...' he mused thoughtfully, then placed one hand on her shoulder and the other under her chin. 'Look into my eyes, Fiona.' He scrutinised her, a frown on his brow. 'I can feel how you tremble. Why is that? Does your heart thud, here, beneath this soft breast?' She remained still as his right hand slid up from her waist and began to caress the swelling curve beneath the thin fabric of her dress. His hand moved to her back, seeking the fastening. She did nothing to assist him. 'Tell me, what will you do when I kiss you? Because I'm going to, even if you don't want me to kiss you. I have the need of your lips, a need forsaken for far too long. And I sense your feelings for me. They haven't quite died, have they, my sweet?' he demanded and, without waiting for her response, he crushed her mouth with his. He began to press his thighs so tightly against hers that she felt his rising passion with some panic. Yet he appeared not to notice her efforts to repel him, merely sliding his free hand down her back to hold her firmly to his body. The kiss went on and on, and suddenly Fiona no longer cared what was happening. She started to answer his movements with her own. For some reason this had the adverse effect on him. He pulled away from her, his eyes bright and enigmatic as he stared down into her flushed, eager face.

Unwisely, she whispered:

'Oh, Alan, I've been such a fool! I shouldn't have let you go.'

'No, you shouldn't. But we can remedy that at once.'

'Then the engagement is on again?' she managed to gasp, her heart full.

He turned from her and leaned across to find a cigarette.

'I thought I'd made myself very clear on that subject. No engagement, no wedding. No, my dear, surely you must have realised what I've been getting at all this time? I find you very desirable and am quite willing to have you as my mistress. When we dock ...' but he got no further.

Fiona had gone chalk-white. She swayed, unable to believe her ears. *Mistress!* Mistress to this man whom she loved so desperately? Surely she had misheard? Alan couldn't have meant those dreadful words?

'I . . . you mean, to live with you without marriage?'

'Of course. I'm not the marrying type.'

'Oh God! God!' she whispered, shaking like a leaf. Her hands were over her face and the tears began to seep through the fingers. She did not see him make a quick movement towards her, control it, and then puff at his cigarette again. Neither did she see the free hand clenched whitely into a balled fist.

When at last she raised her face, her eyes were like large pools in a darkened, purple grotto.

'You insult and humiliate me!' she choked. 'You treat me as filth! How could you! How could you do such a thing to me!' She made for the door and he remained where he was, smoking calmly.

'Before you slam that behind you, one more thing,' his tone was light and firm. 'If you should want to change your mind, come and tell me. I want you, Fiona, remember that.'

The door slammed hard behind her as she stumbled out into the passage. The way back to her cabin was hazy with tears, and fortunately, she found herself alone. For a full half hour she wept out her pain and misery and then climbed into bed, falling into a dreamless sleep almost immediately.

CHAPTER FIVE

FIONA'S pride prevented her from telling Sandra very much about what had taken place between herself and Alan the previous evening, save that he had accepted her apology and the subject was now closed. It was plain that the other girl did not believe her completely, but she asked no further questions. Later, however, she confided her fears to Robert when they were alone, saying that she presumed there to have been a bitter quarrel between Fiona and the captain.

'I rather think you must be right,' Robert sighed. 'I was with him earlier and he was in a filthy mood. Almost flung his cap at me when I made a weak joke about something.'

The two girls went ashore at Tenerife in company with a small group of the other passengers. For Fiona, the sea had lost its cobalt blue, the sky seemed to lower with heat and even the lush subtropical vegetation with its brilliant red, white, blue and yellow flowers failed to stir her heart. She had slept badly and her head ached. She tried to show an interest in her surroundings, and to laugh when the middle-aged gentleman who had latched himself on to her throughout their conducted tour ashore made jokes and teased her about her eyes mirroring the joys and sorrows of Venus herself. On the whole, she was thankful when the time came for them to return aboard and set sail once more for the island of Madeira which would be reached at eight the following morning.

Sandra wanted to dance that evening and would not accept Fiona's excuse, dragging her on to the dance floor where Robert was impatiently awaiting their arrival. He had found chairs for the three of them and helped Fiona into hers, before smiling and saying:

'Forgive me if I whisk her away in this one?'

'Please do.'

'I've ordered long drinks. They should be here in a moment. Goodbye!' He slid an arm about Sandra's waist and drew her close so that his cheek touched her forehead as they danced away across the floor. Fiona stared after them with envy on her face.

Why had she thrown away her chances? she thought with pain. It might have been herself and Alan dancing together. Robert made no secret of his interest in Sandra, she thought, with a slight tremor of a smile on her lips. They were so close they might have been two entwining plants reaching up together for the sunlight.

'Aha!' boomed a voice. 'So there you are, Miss Barclay. 'I'll join you because I see your friend is dancing with the doctor. And where you are, so is she. And,' Mrs Bottlin-Mabee twinkled brashly, 'where she is then I can hope to see our dear, kind doctor.' She flopped down in a chair and then stretched one heavily bejewelled hand across the table. 'Did the doctor buy you these? Good.' She beckoned imperiously to a passing steward and told him brusquely to bring her a gin and tonic.

'Charge it to the doctor, will you, because this is his table.'

Fiona gasped at the sheer audacity of the action, and even the steward raised his eyebrows. Fiona sent him a violent, unspoken message, which he appeared to understand, because he smiled and nodded acquiescence. Fiona's pocket would be the poorer by one gin and tonic. Piggy eyes opposite her almost disappeared under the folds of fat as Mrs Bottlin-Mabee smiled.

'We have nearly three days in Madeira,' she announced. 'I expect you and your nice little friend will be busy sightseeing, won't you? Of course, I have relatives living near Funchal, so I shall be away from the ship during that time. Rather convenient to know all the right people, don't you agree? They like me to visit and always make sure I have everything I want when I want it. Not that I can say the same for this particular cruise liner. I've had to make complaints of one kind or another every day so far. Still, it's the third time I've sailed under Captain Howard, and he's very new at the job, so it's only to be expected, isn't it, that things aren't always as they should be? Mind you, I've given him many hints about the things that are wrong, but he's stubborn and won't listen to friendly advice. Pity, because I shall be putting in a report when I get back. Like I did after travelling to New York about seven years ago. The service was atrocious, so I sent in a five-page report to the shipping line and suggested that the captain should be relieved of his post...'

'And was he?' Fiona asked, the sarcasm of her tone unnoticed by the whalelike figure opposite.

'Unfortunately not. I can't understand why, but I expect he lied and wriggled his way out of trouble. They all do, you know. And probably he had some family interest in the line. Do you happen to know if Captain Howard has any?' she finished eagerly.

As if he had been conjured up by the woman's words, Alan suddenly materialised beside their table. He coughed and both women turned round. At once Mrs Bottlin-Mabee was all smiles and nods.

'Oh, Captain, how nice to see you! Have you come to ask Miss Barclay to dance, because I'm sure it can't be little old me you want as a partner?' She smirked archly at him.

'As a matter of fact, I was hoping to partner both of you. Mrs Bottlin-Mabee?' He held out a hand and the other's pudgy one was thrust into it. 'Miss Barclay,' he was still smiling that humourless smile of his, 'may I have the next with you?' Without waiting for her acquiescence, he added to Mrs Bottlin-Mabee, 'Do you know, I have the feeling that she would run away if she had half the chance.'

I hate you! read Fiona's fierce scowl.

'I won't allow that!' the other woman replied. 'Miss Barclay dear, you just stay there until we get back, and then the dear captain can have his dance with you, just as he said.'

For two pins, Fiona thought in fury as she watched the couple move into the crowd of dancers, I'd get up and go, and to hell with Alan!

But she did not. Robert and Sandra returned after the dance, their arms about each other's waists, and Robert asked Fiona if he might have the next dance with her.

'Thank you.'

Out of the corner of her eye, Fiona saw the massive figure returning with Alan. The dance band struck up once more and Alan held out his hand to Fiona.

'Ours, I think.'

Fiona smiled very sweetly.

'You didn't give me the chance to refuse just now,' she pointed out in sugary tones. 'I was about to tell you I was already promised for this particular dance.' She rose to her feet, looking hopefully at Robert, who seemed rather embarrassed. Smoothly Alan stepped into the breach.

'I'm sure Robert will forgive me on this occasion. I'm afraid I'm due on the bridge in a few moments. Robert?' The doctor nodded and airily waved a hand. With ill grace Fiona allowed herself to be led on to the floor to the rhythm of a slow foxtrot.

'This is more my line,' Alan murmured somewhere in the region of her left ear. 'These modern things make me conscious of my age. All very well for you youngsters, but at my time of life the old bones tend to creak and groan. Don't strain away from me like that!' he scolded, sliding his arm into the small of her back. 'Left thigh against my right, and for heaven's sake look as if you're enjoying it!' He smiled down into her eyes, but there was a strange unreadable message there.

'I didn't want to dance with you, you know!' she said in a pettish tone, pouting. He chuckled with amusement.

'So I gathered. Still, I wanted to dance with *you*, that's why I underwent the torture of having my feet trodden on by the B.-M. woman. Surprised that I came in here for the sole purpose of seeking you out?' She lowered her head and felt his breath fan her cheek. Studiously she studied the centre button of his evening shirt and could feel the strength emanating from him. Her fingers shook a little in his and he gave her a quick, puzzled look.

'Worried, sweetheart?' he asked gently.

'No. Should I be?'

'Perhaps.'

'Why?'

'Because you're afraid you might give in to my demands. No, don't pull away. The others might think we're arguing.'

'We are!' she snapped, her eyes flashing and cheeks red. 'In any case, what makes you think I will give in to your disgusting, despicable, foul . . .'

'Yes?' he asked hopefully, and grinned.

'Oh, I hate you! Demands. Thank God we shall soon be home and I won't have to see or think about you ever again. What bliss that will be!'

'Will it, my love? Won't you be just that tiny bit sorry

you never gave in to me and learned what it is to love a man with your whole body?'

'Stop it! This is neither the time nor the place. Someone might hear.'

'Above this din? Oh, very well. This way.' To her astonishment he steered her neatly out on to the deck where the sky was dark yet warm. Stars glittered like so many diamonds on the glossy black velvet of a swirling cloak. Alan led her some yards along the deck until they were hidden from anyone who might either look out or be strolling past. She heard him laugh.

'Is this better?' His question was gentle. He drew her close and her heart thudded. His lips traced a line along her forehead and then his hand was caressing her neck. 'We have the time and the place. A warm, quiet night ... the stars like gems ... darkness which is warm to the skin ... music coming softly to our ears ... our hearts telling both of us that we yearn for touching hands and lips ... a night of magic and opportunity ...'

With a tiny whimper of surrender Fiona turned her body and raised her head to kiss him. It was not a long embrace, for he put her away from him. She saw the ruffle of his hair in the slight breeze and the glitter of his eyes.

'No, my love, this is too magical. The night would make up your mind for you. When you come to me, I want you on my terms, not those formulated from the intoxication of a subtropical night aboard ship. When the sky is grey, the drizzle penetrating and the sea heaving while the wind blows a sharp coldness into the bones, if you come to me then, I shall have reached the end of my quest.'

'Quest? What quest?'

His forefinger touched the tip of her nose.

'When it happens, I shall tell you. In the meantime, I

must leave you, because up there,' he nodded in the direction of the bridge, 'I have a duty to perform.' He sought her right hand, folded his own over it and then raised it to his lips. The skin seemed to curl with ecstasy as she felt the tip of his tongue caress the back of her hand. 'If you want me, you know where to find me,' he told her.

'Never that!' came the terse reply.

'I wonder. Besides, what does it matter nowadays in this age of permissiveness? Everyone seems to disobey the rules by which I was brought up. So why shouldn't we join them? If you can't beat 'em, join 'em, is the old adage.'

'I have my principles!' she retorted.

'And I, too. But sometimes they can be overruled. Goodnight, Fiona.'

He walked away quickly and her heart thudded madly. Gripping the deck rail, she closed her eyes, the night air hot upon burning cheeks. Oh, God, how desperately she longed to throw everything to the night wind and run after him, begging him to have his will with her! Yet how very shocking to feel like this. It must be, as Alan had said, the intoxication of the subtropics.

She turned to stare up into the sky, her eyes seeing only the firm and determined chin, while the strength of his arms seemed to be about her still. That physical passion should have brought her to this trembling, helpless state! A passion as yet not fully born, but the thoughts were there ... thoughts which burned and tormented in their clarity. Why had she not experienced this frantic yearning and physical torment during those few months when she had first known Alan? Had she been young, too immature? Was it only now, when he no longer wanted to marry her, that she had recognised her own true self? That such a self lurked beneath her normal, placid exterior was rather frightening to learn. And to discover how much the touch of a man could mean was another disturbing element. But she must not give in to the temptations of the flesh! The permissive society was not for her. She would stick to her own principles, or else live a life of shame. No man would take her body unless he had placed a gold band about her finger. She was no bending reed in a wilful wind! She was the upright elm, which stood firm against the storms and tempests. Until, said a tiny voice within, the elm is uprooted and crashes to the ground, while the bending reed continues to wave serenely in the breeze...

She knew she loved Alan more now than in the past, but it was too late. Far, far too late.

She returned to the dance floor where, to her relief, she was delighted to see that Mrs Bottlin-Mabee had been whisked off by a stout and elderly gentleman with long gingery whiskers.

'Robert and I have been discussing tomorrow's arrangements,' Sandra began as Fiona sat down again. 'I hope you don't mind, but he would like us to go to dinner with his friend. Is that all right with you, or were you planning something else?'

'No. I should enjoy dinner ashore very much.' Fiona smiled at Robert's eager face. 'As long as you're sure your kind friend won't object to being saddled with two complete strangers?'

'Nancy is only too pleased for me to bring anyone I like. I've already phoned her on the radio telephone, hoping you two wouldn't have planned something else.' He winked at Sandra. 'In any case, I'd have forced you to come with me, regardless.' Fiona saw the affectionate glances exchanged between them and felt very much alone. Although neither would admit to preferring their own company without

Fiona, she decided to plead tiredness and go to bed. She rubbed her hand across her forehead and said:

'It's very oppressive in here and I've the beginnings of a headache. If it isn't rude of me, would you mind my leaving you now? I'd like to nip this headache in the bud, but if I remain here, with the noise and smoke, I won't succeed. Besides, I want to be at my best to meet your friend Nancy tomorrow.' She picked up her white evening bag and rose from her seat. Robert rose too.

'Can I get you anything?' he asked, his professionalism returning. 'What do you take? I'll send for it from the hospital.'

'I have some Disprin, thank you. I'll take a couple and then turn in. You two enjoy yourselves.'

'I'll be as quiet as a mouse when I come to bed,' Sandra promised as Fiona smiled her goodnights.

Fiona was asleep when Sandra eventually came to bed, but she awoke very early the following morning. She tried to recapture sleep, but it was too elusive. With a sigh, she slid quietly out of bed and threw on a short-skirted cotton dress with a pale pink cardigan. The corridor outside the rows of cabins was quite deserted and there was no one about when she slid back the big door to enter the sports deck. Dawn pointed pink fingers in the east and the breeze brushing her cheek promised another day of balmy heat. With her arms hugging her cardigan about her body, she walked slowly past the paddling pool towards the sun deck. The sound of splashing drew her attention to the main swimming pool. She halted, staring at the swirl of water a few yards away; a swirl which moved rapidly towards the deep end as the unseen swimmer surfaced after a shallow dive. Phosphorescence betrayed the strong arms, and a long trail of glittering silver followed behind like a wake. She saw the swimmer get to his feet, shake his dark head, and the dawn light picking out the paler hue of skin. She could not see his features, and had no idea of his identity, but whoever it was obviously thought he was alone. She began to move away silently, hoping to slip beyond his notice before he looked in her direction. She was too late. His voice rang out:

'George, is that you? Come and have a dip, you lazy devil!'

The voice belonged to Alan. Fiona paused, her body silhouetted against the dawn light. She heard the low whistle, then Alan asked: 'Who's there at this hour of the morning? If you're staff, you know the pool is out of bounds until daylight.'

'Alan, it's me, Fiona,' she replied. She did not want him to think one of the women employed on board had disobeyed the rules. He waded towards the pool's edge, rested his arms on its side, then heaved himself out in one quick springing movement. The sky was lighter now and she could see the water streaming from long legs as he straightened, his hands smoothing back wet hair. Silver gems gleamed as water dripped off his angular form.

'What are you doing here?' he was asking as she watched him. 'Passengers aren't allowed to swim so early.'

'I know. I couldn't get back to sleep.'

'Do you know what the time is?'

'Very early.'

'Yes. And we should be docking in a couple of hours.' He picked up a towel which had been lying on a nearby chair and began to rub his hair with it.

'Do ... do you often take a swim like this?' she asked tentatively, her gaze drawn to the unruly mass of hair which now stood up in a series of blunt spires on the top of his head. She had never seen him like this before, and she was powerless to fight the fascination.

'Whenever I can. I'm not on duty for another hour; otherwise I'd have been on the bridge by now. We dock at eight.' He shifted the towel in one brisk movement, pulling it to and fro across his shoulders. Muscles rippled deep bronze in the half-light. The front of his chest was covered with thick, wet hair. It would take so little just to reach out and touch him ... Hastily she re-clasped her arms and shuddered. Alan stopped towelling and held her shoulder. Again that convulsive shudder.

'You're chilled, my sweet. You should go below and try to get a little more sleep if you can. You have a great deal to see and enjoy when we're in Madeira. Don't forget to have a sleigh ride! They're most exhilarating.' He slung the towel over one arm and prepared to leave her. Fiona was reluctant to let him go, and he seemed to sense this, because he paused, slanting an amused glance at her over one shoulder.

'What will you do when we're at the island?' she asked.

'This and that. Of course, I have various friends I must visit. I can't not do so, because so many of them need only look out of their windows in Funchal to see this liner in the harbour—no possible excuse, you see. I know of one good lady who would be terribly upset if I neglected her.'

Fiona tried to control the surge of jealousy which arose.

'Yes,' she replied in a casual tone, 'I suppose you do have a great many friends, and make more with each cruise.'

'My sweet, much as I enjoy chatting to you like this, I really must make a move. My early morning tea will be waiting for me in my cabin.' He grinned and suggested: 'How about sharing it with me?'

'But the steward will think ...' she began, and bit her lip with fury as flame coursed her face.

'Think you've spent the night with me?' he mirrored her thoughts. 'No such luck, Fiona. He'll have brought it while I've been here with you. And he knows pretty well what I get up to in most of my free time, especially when I leave wet trunks hanging in the shower. So you're quite safe with me. Care to come? We needn't ring for an extra cup. I can use my tooth mug, if you like.'

'It would be outrageous!' she protested. 'I couldn't possibly . . . and besides, look at you! You're not even respectably dressed.'

'I have two cabins, day and night. I'll shut myself firmly in the latter when I dress so you won't need to feel compromised.'

The strange warm tones of the dawn were doing heady things to her. She opened her mouth and almost gave an affirmative answer. What harm could befall her over a cup of tea? Alan was due on duty very soon. Time was on her side and . . . but it would be tempting providence. After his outrageous proposition concerning their joint future, might he not think she was acquiescing if she agreed to join him for tea at this hour? And she did not believe she could trust herself. His nearness now was doing odd things to her. His body smelled of salt from the pool; she could feel the tang of it even though they were separated by a couple of feet. In the cabin there would be electric light; she would see every taut muscle quite clearly. His trunks were shockingly brief. It would be the first time in her life that he had worn so little while in her company. She did not trust herself to behave properly. Even if he went straight into his night cabin to dress, she would see him standing there like some lean Greek god. It was not fair to her. Her resolve could crumble . . . principles float away like the wake behind this liner . . .

'Thank you, Alan, but I think I'd prefer to return to my

own cabin for my tea,' she said in a slightly shaky voice.

'Please yourself.' He strode away without another glance.

Deeply disturbed by the tumult within her, Fiona remained on the sun terrace for a further ten minutes, watching the sun rise in all its scarlet glory before returning to her cabin where she found her companion still peacefully asleep.

Most of the passengers appeared to be disembarking for a busy day ashore. Chattering and laughing in their little groups, they streamed off the ship. Sandra had arranged to wait for Robert, so they were some of the last passengers to leave. Idly Fiona looked around, her thoughts on Alan. She hoped she might see him, but while many of the crew were also going ashore, she was unable to spot him. She craned her neck to stare up at the bridge, but she was too far in its lee to see anyone.

'Sorry I'm late!' Robert greeted them cheerfully, a special smile for Sandra. Fiona felt she was *de trop*, and the feeling persisted throughout the entire day, although neither Sandra nor Robert showed in any way that they considered her presence a burden.

Robert found a taxi which drove them slowly through the busy Avenida Arriaga, the main thoroughfare of Funchal, the island's capital. Both girls exclaimed their delight at the sight of so much bright colour and beauty. The pavements were formed of intricate black and white mosaic, while down the centre of the avenue, the fresh green jacaranda trees stabbed the air with their violet blue flowers.

'Coffee?' Robert asked.

'Please!' Fiona and Sandra chorused in unison, then laughed.

The taxi stopped near the cathedral, where there was a gay, open market peopled with women in scarlet-striped skirts, red capes and dazzling white blouses. There was a profusion of flowers everywhere. Robert stopped at a stall and spoke to one of the women who wore a tiny black skull-cap from which sprouted a tail. Fiona could not draw away her eyes from this lovely island costume. He bought two small sprays of bright blue flowers and gave them to his companions, bestowing a kiss on Fiona's cheek and another on Sandra's eager mouth.

'I expect they'll wither before we get back to the ship later today,' he declared happily, sliding Sandra's hand into his. 'And now for coffee, after which I expect you'll both want to purchase wicker baskets and see some of the beautiful embroidery done by the country women of the island.'

The day seemed to fly past and soon they were on their way to Terreiro da Luta, which was almost three thousand feet above sea level.

'This is it,' Robert grinned, pointing to a huge wicker basket which looked like a laundry basket for giants. The two men in wide straw hats standing beside the basket beamed back. 'In you get, you two. Sandra, you sit next to Fiona and I'll be on your other side.' They climbed into the comfortable conveyance and waited for the ride to begin. The basket was mounted on sturdy wooden runners while the two men in boaters controlled the rate of descent with ropes attached to these runners. The pace increased to almost breakneck speed as they swept over the steep, twisting cobblestone roads. Fiona's heart lurched as the man on her side of the sleigh leapt on to the runner and grinned down at her. She glanced quickly to the far side and the second man was also sharing their ride. She wondered how on earth they could control this thing rushing and swooshing over cobbles, narrowly missing the corners and careering down the steep slopes back towards Funchal. But the men obviously knew what they were doing, for within moments of travelling with them on the sleigh, they were back on the road, the ropes taut and firm, controlling the speed of descent with their own backward tilt of body and running legs.

When the ride was over, Fiona ran a hand through dishevelled hair.

'Oh, that was wonderful, if a little scary!'

'You should have called out to slow down,' Robert teased.

'But I don't speak any Portuguese at all!' she protested.

'Nevertheless, they'd have understood you.' Robert glanced down at his wristwatch and told them that it was time they returned to the ship if they were not to be late in preparing for their dinner engagement. He found a taxi with ease and soon they were passing through the busy city centre once more.

Sandra could not make up her mind what to wear. She dithered between a soft linen dress with a low neckline and swirling, fluted sleeves and a pale blue creation which was devastating in its simplicity. Fiona knew it must have cost the earth. It fitted Sandra like a glove. She brushed her hair, patting the waves until they curled into the nape of her neck. She turfed out the contents of her small jewellery box to select something suitable to wear around her neck.

'What do you think?' she asked, holding up a slender gold chain on which hung an old English guinea set in delicate filigree gold.

'Lovely!'

'I have a guinea bracelet to match as well. David gave them to me. His father collected guineas and he had them made up like this for our first wedding anniversary. Poor David! He would have enjoyed this kind of cruise.'

Fiona's dress was also simple. Its attraction lay in the

pastel shade of honey-gold and the superb cut of the fabric. Unlike Sandra's this dress had no sleeves, while the bodice was cut very tight so that the swoop of neckline revealed part of Fiona's cleavage between the upper portions of her firm breasts. The skirt was very full and the hem perfectly even. Her pantyhose were sheer and the pumps she had thrust on her feet were exactly right. She had thought of putting up her hair and decided against this. She had added a faint touch of eye-shadow, but the lipstick she had chosen did not match at all, and she was now in the process of scrubbing it off. It would have to be a coral shade after all. The tan of the sun shouted at the golden shade originally chosen.

At last they were ready to leave. Each girl carried a light coat over one arm. Robert had promised to meet them at the carpeted main entrance. When they arrived, Robert was not alone, and Fiona's heart missed a beat. Immaculate in evening dress, Alan stood beside the doctor. He smiled first at Sandra and then at Fiona.

'I forgot to tell you,' Robert said in a cheerful tone, 'Alan always joins me when I visit Nancy. She'd never forgive either of us if he didn't call when we're on the island. Sandra?' He held out his hand and she went to his side, leaving Fiona to stare foolishly at Alan. His face was bland and there was something in his eyes which she could not define.

'Going to run away while you can?' he asked in a mocking tone.

'Certainly not!'

'Good. Then it's a truce for this evening?'

'No truce. Merely that good manners prohibits any animosity in front of a lady to whom I haven't yet been introduced.'

'But you're surprised to see me, aren't you?'

'Yes, although I suppose I ought to have guessed, because you and Robert are such good friends.'

'Shall we go? The others will be waiting.' He took her arm.

An elderly but beautifully kept limousine of some obscure European make was parked on the quay, and its chauffeur stepped forward to open the rear door with a grand flourish, his face wreathed in smiles.

'How are you, Joseph?' Alan asked as he paused before helping Fiona into the vehicle.

'Very well indeed, thank you, sir. The parcel has been brought from the ship and I have it safely with me in front.'

'Good. Your mistress?'

'Very well indeed, sir, thank you.'

'I'm glad to hear it.'

There was ample room for all four of them on the rear seat. Fiona wanted to giggle at such vastness when she had been used to crushing herself into small, more economical cars. This was rather like a second-class Rolls-Royce, although the interior was just as luxurious, with real leather seats which seemed to have been cunningly fashioned for the passenger's body. The chauffeur started the engine and they were off, travelling swiftly through the city, making for the heights above.

'Where are we going?' Sandra asked as they passed large white houses with red-tiled roofs.

'Nancy's house is less than a mile from here,' Robert explained. 'She has one of the best views in Funchal. And she prides herself on the beauty of her garden.'

Fiona was very conscious of Alan's thigh against hers. At first she had tried to edge away from him but, although there had been room for all of them on the seat, there was none for untoward movement. She glanced down at the smartly tailored leg, her gaze travelling to his well-polished shoes, while the warmth of his left arm permeated the tiny jacket she wore over her sleeveless dress. Daring to glance at his face, she found him regarding her with amusement in his darkly flecked eyes. Suddenly the amusement was replaced by an entirely different expression; one that seemed to burn through her. She trembled and felt the reassuring nudge of his knee before his hand closed over hers, long fingers intertwining in such a gentle way that she almost choked with emotion, and yearned to bury her face in his wide chest and weep her heart out.

The drive leading from the road to the big white house was twisting, giving the impression of being longer than it really was. The limousine purred to a halt and Joseph sprang out to fling open the rear door, handing out his female passengers with an oddly old-fashioned courtesy which Fiona found touching and delightful. She smiled at him and was rewarded with a bright twinkle from sharp eyes. Sandra leaned close to whisper mischievously,

'Now I know what it's like to be Royalty!'

Fiona was impatient to meet Joseph's employer, wondering if she, too, had retained much old-world charm. She glanced towards him as he spoke to Alan.

'Your parcel, sir. Shall I bring it into the house for you?'

'No, thank you, Joseph. I'll take it myself.'

'Very good, sir.' With an almost Teutonic click of his heels, he handed Alan an average-sized brown paper parcel that had been carefully tied with string. Alan tucked it under his arm and Fiona found herself being curious as to its contents.

The front door was opened at their approach, almost as if someone had been peering through a peephole in anticipation of their arrival. A tiny, white-haired woman in a crisp grey linen dress beamed with delight at the two men and then bobbed to the girls. She bade them all a good evening before she showed them into the house. She turned to Robert.

'The mistress is waiting in the lounge for you, Master Robert. You're looking fine, if you don't mind my saying so, so I can see you're fit and well.'

'I'm splendid, thank you, Aenone. And what about you?' Robert caught her shoulders and gave her an affectionate kiss. 'Still my very own girl, I see.'

She laughed and gave him a friendly little push.

'Oh, get away with you, Master Robert! Teasing and joking like you always do. And you, Master Alan,' she peered at him through narrowed eyes. 'Not looking quite so well as last time. Not been poorly, I hope?'

Fiona's eyes shot towards Alan's face and her heart skipped a beat. Did he look unwell? Why had she not noticed for herself? But Alan was smiling warmly back at Aenone.

'No, my dear, I'm perfectly fit, I'm pleased to say. Perhaps just a little overtired, nothing more. It will be a busy summer season, I think.'

'So much responsibility being in charge of big boats,' Aenone nodded. 'Even though you have all those electronic gadget things to stare at, someone still has to hold the tiller, of course.'

Alan grinned widely.

'Certainly. However, my officers do occasionally allow me a little time off to snatch forty winks. And my electronic gadgets can be relied upon to tell us when something might not be quite right. No, it's the passengers who cause me real lack of sleep.' He winked at Sandra. 'Especially some of the ladies.'

'Beast!' Sandra whispered in a low tone, but his eyes had flickered towards Fiona with such a fire in their depths that she had to bite her lip and turn away.

'This way, please,' said Aenone, hurrying across the wide, airy hall towards a big closed door. As she followed the bustling little woman, Fiona could not help wondering about Nancy. What kind of woman was she to have an elderly retainer who treated grown men with such familiarity, and as if they had still been small boys in short trousers?

Aenone opened the big door and went inside, where they heard her say to the room's occupant, 'The boys are here, Madam.'

Alan reached for Fiona's hand and led her into a cool lounge. It was so delightfully furnished that it almost took her breath away. Brilliantly polished furniture, cool venetian blinds whose slats had been raised so that the full glory of the garden with the distant panorama of Funchal could be seen. The scent of flowers was heavy inside the room. Vases of blooms on every available table and shelf.

It was not, however, the room or the garden which caught more than that first fleeting glance; it was the diminutive yet commanding figure of a woman seated in a high-backed chair. Although deeply lined, her face was lovely, with huge violet eyes which smiled warmly at her guests. Her skin was like a baby's in texture, and when she smiled, her teeth were perfect. To Fiona, she seemed a strange mixture of youth and age; time had treated her gently, retaining the very best of both eras.

'Nancy, it's good to see you!' Alan declared, striding swiftly towards her. He bent down and kissed her while two frail, badly deformed hands reached up to clasp him about the neck. Fiona hid her dismay as she saw the cruel effects of arthritis in those gentle hands.

'Dear boy! My dear, dear boy. I'm always so impatient to see you. And you, too, you young rogue,' Nancy added as Alan stepped aside for Robert to come over and kiss her cheek. The arms went round his neck and once again she murmured: 'Dear boy!'

'Nancy, we've brought two friends,' said Robert, turning to extend his hand to Sandra who now stepped forward shyly. 'This is Sandra Stern. Now you be nice to her, because I'm going to marry her and I don't want you frightening her away by those appalling stories about me.'

The violet eyes searched Sandra's rosily blushing face and then her hands were clasped in the stiff ones.

'Yes, you have chosen well, Robert. You may kiss me if you wish, child.' Sandra obeyed without hesitation. The wide eyes looked beyond Sandra to Fiona and a frown appeared on Nancy's forehead. 'And who is this, Alan? I feel that we have met before. Have we, my dear?'

'I'm afraid not.' Fiona came to the chair and held out one hand, but Nancy took both in the same warm grip she had given Sandra. Alan was at her side.

'Nancy, allow me to introduce Fiona.'

Realisation dawned in the older woman's eyes and she nodded.

'Then we have met before—through Alan's words. You are *the* Fiona.'

Cold fingers clutched Fiona's spine. What did Nancy mean? That Alan had discussed her intimately with their hostess? She did not have to answer Nancy because Alan slid his arm about her waist and spoke reassuringly.

'Yes, Nancy, this is the Fiona I used to know. The girl I was hoping to bring to you ...'

Fire coursed through the younger girl's face and she

wanted to tear herself from Alan and hide alone with her embarrassment. She darted a fulminating glance towards Alan who seemed perfectly composed as he continued.

'It was a pleasant surprise to have her aboard after such a long time. Naturally she didn't know I was the captain, otherwise I fear she might not have sailed with me. Isn't that so, my dear?' He smiled into Fiona's eyes, but there was no mirth there. 'However, for everyone's sake, we decided to call a truce. At least, until the cruise is over, when I suppose we shall be back to the old terms again.'

Nancy's gaze darted swiftly from one to the other and a little frown marred her forehead.

'By old terms, my sweet,' Alan purred at Fiona, 'I mean the parting of the ways. In the meantime, we're just good friends, Nancy, that's all.'

'You're embarrassing Fiona!' Nancy snapped in obvious disapproval. 'I'll have no petty quarrels in my house. I suggest we discuss another topic.' Her tone softened as she turned to Fiona, reaching again for her hands to squeeze them gently. 'Any friend of Robert's and Alan's is welcome in my house, my dear. You must put Alan's churlish remark down to overtiredness, I think. Alan, my boy, did you manage all that shopping I asked for?'

'Of course. Everything you wanted from Marks. If something isn't quite right, then send Joseph down to the ship tomorrow, and I'll get it changed for you when I'm back home. Aenone, no doubt, will have unpacked the parcel and spread everything out for your inspection later tonight.'

'Thank you, Alan. Are you sure you had sufficient money to cover it all? I know how swiftly prices alter these days.'

'All perfectly square.'

Nancy beamed at Fiona who was listening to this exchange with considerable astonishment.

'I may be getting on for eighty, but I still have a soft spot for really good, pretty lingerie. None of your old thick vests and red-flannel-type drawers for me, thank you!' Everyone laughed. 'I like to treat myself to the luxury of soft silky things next to my skin. Of course, living in a hot climate like this, at times nylon isn't always advisable, but as I seldom go out, I don't get overheated, therefore I tend to indulge myself disgracefully.' She chuckled. 'I'm sure my neighbours enjoy themselves hugely with guessing games as to which of us wears the frilly nonsense they see fluttering on the clothes line! I rely on Alan to buy what I need. He seems to know exactly what I like. I often think of him asking the women assistants for dainty things and visualise him blushing to the roots of his hair. The dear boy!' She gazed at him fondly and he patted her hand.

'The "dear boy" as you put it, Nancy, rushes through the lingerie department of any big store as if he were born to it. I rifle the racks of hanging nonsense, select what I want, hold it up to the light, slide my hands inside and feel the texture and then beam at the nearest lady customer, who's terribly shocked when I wink and tell her it's for my favourite girl-friend.' He grinned at the girls who stared at him, open-mouthed. 'There you are, you see, just like these two prim young ladies. Visions of a luscious eyeful hidden in a love nest ... No, I overstep the mark. Forgive me, Nancy, I'm being crude, and that isn't necessary at all. I've made our two girls blush, so I'll change the subject hastily, or else retire to the garden to hide my confusion. May I pour the drinks, or shall Robert do so?'

Robert was already moving to the table in the corner of the room while Nancy shook her head.

'Incorrigible! I'll overlook it just this once. And how are you both enjoying the cruise? I hope you've been blessed with excellent sailing weather, with no queasiness?' The three women then embarked on a lively discussion.

It was only when Aenone arrived to announce that dinner was ready that Fiona realised the full extent of Nancy's disability. Both men rose at once, but Alan reached her side first, with a wink at Robert and the words: 'My turn today.' He bent over her, slid one arm behind her knees and the other at her back, and then lifted her as easily as if she had been thistledown. 'Comfy?' Their eyes were level. Nancy smiled.

'Beautifully, thank you.'

'Right.' Alan strode purposefully out of the room while Nancy turned to beam back at the girls who were following, one on either side of Robert.

'I like to be pampered by my boys,' she confided happily. 'When I know they're coming, I get Aenone to banish my horrid wheelchair into some dark recess. I'm sure she scolds it as she does so!' They all laughed.

Dinner was a great success, their hostess sparkling with gaiety and warmth. Fiona watched her carefully and it did not take long before she realised that both Alan and Robert adored the old lady, cherishing her as if she were their own grandmother, and behaving almost like a couple of broody hens. Later, after coffee and liqueurs had been served and drunk, Nancy sent Robert and Sandra into the garden to admire the new flowering shrub she had had planted in a border at the eastern end.

'You two can go and look later,' she told Alan firmly as he began to make a tentative move after the couple. 'I'm surprised at you! Surely it's more than obvious that dear Robert can't wait to be alone with that pretty child? Especially if he's going to marry her.'

'There's nothing definite yet,' Fiona ventured.

'Nonsense! He said so when he arrived, didn't he? In any case, my dear, their eyes give them away.' Nancy nodded with satisfaction. 'I can always tell with young people. And slightly older ones, too. Alan, remind me to tell that dear boy not to dilly-dally too long, won't you? No good ever came of procrastination . . . or other things.' She stared pointedly at Fiona, who reddened and began to feel extremely uncomfortable. 'Alan!'

'Yes, my dear?'

'There's a book I wanted you to have. It's in the study. Before either of us forgets, run along and fetch it now, will you, please?'

Thus rather peremptorily dismissed, Alan left the room and Fiona was alone with Nancy. The latter patted the chair nearest her own and ordered:

'Sit by me. I very much would like a private talk with you.' Fiona obeyed, folding her skirts carefully about her legs while the sharp eyes watched. 'I know it's none of my business, of course, but at my age you can be excused for being a meddlesome old thing. At least, that's the excuse I give when I know I'm about to poke my nose where probably its presence is unwelcome—one of the privileges of reaching the late seventies and not being in full command of one's limbs. Compensation therefore must be full. So I interfere dreadfully and, I assure you, it's great fun because none of my friends dare answer me back or tell me to mind my own business. They think I'm a gorgon, but one to be humoured, fortunately.' She smiled gently. 'And my two boys are quite cowed by me.' She laughed at the astonishment now showing on Fiona's face. 'Don't worry, dear. Alan can take a hint. He'll have to spend at least half an hour looking at a very boring book before he dare set foot in here again. He should have guessed what I'd be about.

In fact, I'm certain he knows; therefore it really was just that little bit naughty of him not to warn you in advance. He knew as soon as I saw you two together, I'd want to question you.'

Fiona cast a frantic look at that closed door, but Nancy's crippled hand touched her forearm.

'Please, dear, I'm rude and overbearing, but curiosity burns me up. I'm so terribly fond of Alan ... You see, child, I lost my husband many years ago and, although he left me very comfortably off—he was in wines, you see, and Portuguese—we were never blessed with babies of our own, a great sorrow to us both. I can't recall how many years ago it was that I met those two dear boys, and it matters little. I do know how badly you hurt my dear Alan by breaking off the marriage, because he was terribly in love with you. He's normally a reticent man, but I heard all about it. He had no one else to talk to, you understand. He was wounded and deeply humiliated. Yes, my dear, now you can blush and hang your head while I note the dampness of a tear upon your cheek. Wipe it away, child! This is no time for feminine weaknesses! Ever since you arrived, I've been watching you covertly. I'm no fool, even if I am in my dotage. You're still very much in love with him, yet something holds you back. What is it? Do you trust an interfering old busybody sufficiently to tell me all about it?'

Nancy's face was alive with compassion and Fiona suddenly realised that she was a woman who inspired confidences. She took a deep breath and soon the whole unhappy tale was pouring from her lips. Nancy listened without comment until Fiona ended chokingly,

'He—he doesn't want me any more.'

'Nonsense!'

Fiona was surprised at the scorn in the older woman's tone.

'It's true. He said so. He doesn't want a wife now. He wants ... he just wants me, as I am. No ring, no trappings, no marriage.'

After a very long pause, Nancy remarked, 'I see. I suppose it's only what I should have expected. He was most emphatic after the broken engagement in his conviction that he would never marry. I'm afraid, my dear, you have a great deal to answer for.'

Fiona bit her lip. 'I know. But it's too late to put back the clock. Besides, I really was awfully silly in my attitude. I behaved like a child, not an adult.'

'The decision you now have to make is, are you going to surrender to Alan?' Fiona blushed. 'Oh, don't mind me, child! I may be old, but I'm not entirely ignorant of all that goes on in this modern world. Alan wants to make love to you without the formality of a wedding-ring. He's left the decision to you, so what are you going to do about it?'

'I...I...'

'You have principles?'

'Of course. But I love him so much!' The words came on a thin wail of unhappiness. 'There are times when I almost give in, then I suffer agonies of conscience afterwards because I know I shall be doing wrong.'

'Would you take an old woman's advice?'

'Gladly.'

'Then go to him. Tell him you agree to his proposal and then wait to see what happens.'

'Give in? Just like that? Become his mistress? Cast aside every moral principle with which I've been brought up? I don't know how I can. You see, after I've given in, I have to live with myself. What do I do when he tires of me? I should be so ashamed of myself and I couldn't bear that. I know you think I'm weak, that I want the best of two worlds, but I shall be degrading myself by becoming his mistress. The temptation is there, of course, and I find it hard to resist when I'm feeling down in the dumps. Yet I'm utterly convinced that if I go to Alan, it has to be for always.'

'Exactly!' came the enigmatic declaration. 'Take my advice and offer yourself on the altar of maidenly sacrifice ... there, I've brought a smile to your eyes at long last.' Nancy leaned forward to touch Fiona's cheek with her lips. 'I like you, my dear. Alan has chosen well. You've wasted three precious years; don't waste any more, I beg of you. Even when you falter, think of this last: remember, I *know* Alan! Take your courage in both hands and go to him, no matter how hard it is. He needs you so much. Ah, just in time. Here comes the gentleman in question. Alan, did you find that book?'

Fiona turned away her face, hoping her fiery cheeks had cooled and that he would not notice the over-brightness of her eyes.

'Yes, Nancy, I did. However,' Alan's smile broadened, 'I think you must have made a mistake because I don't read that kind of literature. So I put on my thinking-cap and reasoned that you wanted to have Fiona to yourself for about half an hour; therefore I stayed away until sheer boredom drove me back to this room. Nancy's like that, Fiona, very possessive. When she sets her heart on having her own way, there's no stopping her. I hope you two had a nice little chat and that she didn't run me down too much? Her favourite topic, telling others about the misdeeds of her two "boys".' He was talking too fast, Fiona realised, much too fast in order to cover his embarrassment. Her cheeks reddened once more. Was it possible he *knew* Nancy had wanted to talk about the past? To learn Fiona's side of the broken affair?

At that moment Robert and Sandra returned from the garden and the conversation continued in a light and happy vein. Fiona waited on tenterhooks, suspecting that Nancy might try to throw Alan and her together. It was not long before the older woman put her suggestion.

'Alan, I do want you to see how beautifully my new shrub has bloomed. It's almost dark, so take Fiona with you while you both can still see.'

'Its scent is delicious,' Sandra put in with enthusiasm. 'I only wish it were possible to take a cutting home, but Robert tells me the shrub would wither and die in the harsher climate of England.'

'Yes,' Nancy agreed. 'It would be unfair to try. Unless, of course, you had a hot-house, but then it might die through not being in the open air. Off you go, you two.'

Fiona felt decidedly uncomfortable with Alan strolling at her side. She made an attempt at bright conversation, but the words just would not come to mind. A long silence ensued.

'Well?' he said at last, sarcasm in his tone. 'Did you pick me to pieces satisfactorily? Don't deny I was under discussion, because both my ears were on fire. Knowing you, no doubt you had some pat sob-story ready at your finger tips to explain why you broke our engagement, but you won't have fooled Nancy. She's far too astute to be taken in by your innocent eyes. Now where do you think you're going?' he demanded roughly, grabbing her arm as she turned to run from him in distress.

'Back to the house. I didn't come out here just to be

insulted and mocked.'

'You'll stay here with me, until we've duly sniffed the perfume of Nancy's prize shrub.' His hold was relentless. 'Believe me, my sweet, it doesn't really matter one way or the other to me what you told Nancy. She'll have nothing said against either Robert or myself. Even if we carried off the crime of the century by stealing the Crown Jewels, she wouldn't believe it. Now, are you going to walk quietly beside me, because we're almost there?'

She kept her face averted while the lump in her throat seemed to choke her. How could she bring herself to tell this hard, cruel man that she was willing to be his mistress? Nancy had been mistaken. Alan would not respond kindly, of that she was absolutely certain.

They had reached the corner of the garden where the shrub had been planted. Delicate pink flowers hung on slender stems while the evening air was filled with an almost heady scent. As if he read her thoughts, Alan leaned close to her ear and whispered,

'This perfume speaks of love—wild, passionate love. Do you not sense its mystery in the air?' His tone softened almost seductively and she shivered. Alan stood so close she only had to incline her own body that fraction of an inch towards his and the contact would set the seal to what she instinctively believed must be her final surrender.

But not here! Not in the garden! If she allowed him to kiss her, to hold her ... despite their angry words, his attraction was almost overwhelming ... here, under the darkening sky ...

No, Nancy had not meant it that way!

Fiona made a little sound deep in her throat and he turned to face her, his eyes glittering strangely.

'What's happened to you these past three years?' he

whispered. 'So gauche, unsure, innocent and virginal. Now a true woman, one poised on the threshold of life's greatest mysteries: the joy of surrender to love. Come my sweet, let's pretend, shall we? Let's pretend we're madly in love with each other. Let's forget the unhappinesses of the past and surrender to the present with this perfume driving us both mad, as if we'd drunk too much wine.' His thumbs pressed remorselessly into her upper arms. 'We'll throw discretion to the winds. We'll forget who we are. I shall forget I'm the captain of a cruise ship while you forget you're a timid, scared little lamb. We'll remember only that we love each other just for this moment. Above all, my love, I *want* you.' She struggled to break free, but his body kept her prisoner as his hot breath seemed to sear her mouth when he lowered his head. 'Nancy knew what she was doing, sending us out here together. She knew what might happen if I held you like this. And you also knew, because she told you . . .'

'No . . . no!'

Alan laughed unkindly.

'Yes, you did. Try denying you're as hungry for me as I am for you. That you've become a full-blooded woman. That you . . .'

'Stop it! Stop it!' she wept, but he continued without pause.

'No matter what happens in the future, you will never be allowed to forget for one moment that you're mine. Only mine. Even if you find some other man fool enough to want to marry you, the memory of my face and this evening beside the bushes will come flooding back to you. My beloved . . . my love . . . my mistress!'

His mouth swooped on hers as she let out a strangled cry. Their lips touched fleetingly, but somehow she was free of him. Free and backing quickly away while he stood and watched her, a little smile twisting his lips.

'You're a beast! An animal! How dare you treat me like ... like ...'

'A woman of the streets?' he put in harshly. 'Surely that's where a man usually finds a mistress?'

She pressed her hand across her mouth and ran blindly away from him.

Three minutes later, he came across Fiona's dejected figure slumped in a garden seat. She was aware of his presence but did not look up or attempt to evade him a second time. He sat down at her side and placed one hand on her knee. She shivered and cringed from him. He winced.

'Do you hate me that badly?' he whispered. 'I'm sorry. Perhaps I deserved it after all those terrible things I said. I didn't mean them.'

'Yes, you did. At the time,' she pointed out in a low, unhappy tone.

'I wonder. Was I merely goading you because of my own painful memories?' He shrugged wryly. 'I'm afraid I shall never know. And we two are supposed to have a truce!'

'So I thought.'

'Which explains why it's so simple for nations to resume belligerency one with another. If two supposedly decent people can't be together without cruel words and vile bickering, then how can anyone expect sophisticated nations to behave? Let me see your face.' He reached for her chin to turn her head towards him. This time she did not cringe because his fingers were soft and gentle. 'Your eyes are a little red, but I don't think anyone will notice. However, shall we stroll a little further around this beautiful garden before returning to Nancy and the others?'

'I feel more composed now, thank you.'

'Good. I shall indeed honour the terms of our truce from now on. No more vicious accusations or cruel words. Please try to forgive and forget all I said, will you?'

'I...I...'

'I know what you're trying to say. It's easy to ask someone to forgive and forget, but nearly impossible for that person to do so. Time may blur the edge of harsh words, but they still have the unfortunate habit of ringing loudly in the mind. Like painful events, they're persistent in their returning. Now, a truce should always be sealed by both parties.' He heard her sudden indrawn breath and smiled gently into her eyes. 'No, my love, I won't risk the obvious for fear I might be led astray. Give me your right hand, please.' Slowly she lifted it and Alan took it, covering it with both his own.

'From this moment on, I shall abide by the terms we agreed. We are good friends, nothing more. I promise not to break my word, although I want you to feel free at any time to break yours, should you so wish it.'

'Why?' she asked, puzzled, and there was a hint of mischief in his eyes.

'I want you to trust me, to feel you can talk to me about anything, no matter how deeply it may affect you. I want you, my love.' The final words were so softly spoken that she was not sure she had heard correctly. He raised her hand to his lips and kissed the back of it. Her finger curled within his hold as her nerves danced excitedly. He appeared not to have noticed her involuntary reaction. He helped her to her feet.

'Come, let's walk on and then return to the house.'

It was eleven o'clock before Joseph was summoned to drive them back to the dockside. Fiona was genuinely sorry to have to say goodbye to her new friend and, when she leaned to kiss the papery cheek, Nancy whispered;

'I don't really think it can be goodbye, for that is so final. Just remember my advice. Put him out of his misery, dear. He's not at all himself these days.'

Fiona cast an involuntary glance at Alan who, fortunately, was in conversation with Robert and did not overhear the low tones of his hostess. Nancy next kissed Sandra and wished both her and Robert every happiness for the future, insisting that she be one of the very first to know when the engagement was made public.

'Even if you have to send me an S.O.S., or whatever it is you seamen radio ashore from sea.'

'Hardly a distress call, Nancy!' Robert chuckled. 'Otherwise we'd have all the rescue services this side of the Atlantic flocking out to sea.' Nancy twinkled back.

'An engagement is no distress call, I agree,' she laughed. 'It's a time for great happiness and joy.' Her gaze flickered towards Alan who stood nearby, his mouth set in a hard line.

'In any case, my dear,' Robert continued, holding the blushing Sandra close to his side, 'I believe it might be more ethical to tell her parents before we splash the news all over the oceans.'

'You promise to bring her back to see me as soon as you're married?' the old woman demanded imperiously. 'I shall be waiting with much impatience. It's a long time since ...' She broke off swiftly and smiled up at Alan as he leaned from his great height to bestow a kiss upon her forehead. She clasped his hand and stared into his eyes.

'Be gentle, my dear,' she told him a very low tone. 'Act wisely, too. Above all, remember that your own pain cannot be assuaged by deliberately trying to injure others.'

Fortunately Fiona heard nothing of this quick exchange,

although Robert was close enough to hear part, and he frowned before glancing swiftly from Fiona to Alan, and then gave a slight shrug as if to imply that people in love certainly behaved irrationally at times.

The darkness inside the limousine was warm and, once again, Fiona was terribly aware of Alan's thigh pressed against hers. A sudden sense of forgiveness swept over her and she laid one hand on his knee. She felt his initial jolt of astonishment, then his fingers began to stroke the back of her hand, the thumb steady in its hard pressure.

After a while, the strange magic of the night and the purr of the car's engine seemed to lull her into a state of blissful contentment. She turned her head towards Alan's, only to find him watching her, his breath fanning the bridge of her nose.

Oh, Alan! Alan! her heart whispered in tumult. If only we could forget the cruelty of the past!

With a sigh, she leaned against his chest and his lips tumbled her hair.

She wanted the drive to go on and on, its magic leading to some kind of fulfilment of a dream. But it could not be. It ended all too quickly and they were standing in the night, bidding a friendly goodnight to Joseph, who wished them a good and happy cruise.

Fiona did not speak as they re-embarked. Alan no longer held her hand. He was once again the captain, coming aboard after an evening ashore. His back was straight and held erect. He seemed suddenly to be very distant from her.

CHAPTER SIX

THE night seemed interminable. Fiona tossed and turned in her bed, longing for the weary hours to pass, but her mind would not let her rest. Even though she closed her eyes tight, bright images of the evening swam vividly in front of her, and seemed so real that she felt she could reach out and touch Alan and Nancy. Again and again she heard Alan's unkind mockery and his plea to her to forget he had ever said such terrible things. Then Nancy's gentle face rose before her, her lips mouthing the words that boomed through her head; wait and see what happens.

She seemed to be suspended between sleep and wakefulness. She was shouting at Alan while Nancy stood by, wringing her hands and crying out in despair:

'No, my dear, that is *not* the way!'

The following morning Fiona awoke with a dull headache and deep shadows under her eyes. Even Sandra came down from her cloud of happiness sufficiently to comment on her friend's wan appearance.

'I expect that marvellous dinner at Nancy's just didn't agree with me,' Fiona confessed at last when eventually bullied into giving some explanation for her present forlorn state.

'In that case, Bob must see you. At once.' Sandra reached for the phone as Fiona began to protest.

'Please don't—I feel such a fraud. There's nothing wrong with me, I promise.' But Sandra refused to listen and Fiona felt very foolish indeed when Robert arrived, complete with little bag, to sit on the edge of her bed and ask questions about her digestion, and how many times she had been sick during the night. Fiona laughed.

'Honestly, not once, I promise!'

'Then you're feeling queasy? Hot climates often play strange games with one's innards, you know.'

'Not even the teeniest bit queasy. I'm sorry to disappoint you.'

'Hm!' Robert remarked, and reached for her wrist to feel her pulse. 'Perfectly normal. What about temperature?' That also proved unremarkable. 'Then there's only one thing I can suggest.'

'Yes?' Sandra replied eagerly from behind him. He turned to study her with mock severity.

'Madam, are you the patient?'

'No,' Sandra giggled.

'Then kindly leave the professional man to his job. I recommend some fresh rolls, a strong cup of coffee, a cool dress, a comfy deckchair set in a warm but sheltered spot on the deck for an hour or two, after which you'll be your old self again and will be ready to accompany us on a drive around the island.'

'Oh no, I couldn't intrude. You and Sandra want to be alone.'

'No, we don't,' came the latter's firm denial. 'Bob's promised to take me to see the place where Sir Winston Churchill used to paint years ago. And, being British like me, you mustn't miss this opportunity. Let me find a suitable dress and then nip out to grab a good spot on deck. I could do with a nice sit-down for an hour or so myself. So much excitement after a long spell of illness! Bob only said last night that he thought I could be overdoing it, isn't that so, darling?'

'Yes. But what she really means,' he grinned, 'is that I won't be free until after lunch and she doesn't want to go ashore without me.'

'Such conceit!' Sandra added fondly.

'Any excuse, you see. Sandra, ring for your coffee and rolls, will you? I must be on my way. I fear rather a few ladies appear to have overindulged yesterday and now require my expertise.' He went to the door. 'See you at about one-thirty, all right? By the way, I'm now on my way to our august captain who has requested my services.'

'Oh?' Fiona glanced quickly at him. 'What's wrong? Not unwell, I hope?'

'Sheer bad temper, if you ask me. A bear with a sore head. Something's got under his skin to annoy him, like as not. Goodbye. See you both after lunch. I think I shall have to prescribe a full glass of soothing Madeira for Alan and a quick turn about the deck where, with luck, he might find two young ladies of very pleasing appearance to cheer him up and kick away the doldrums.'

Sitting in her deckchair, Fiona began to doze off. She could not help wondering what had upset Alan, although instinctively she realised that she was the cause of his bad mood. Her eyelids closed and she drifted off into a refreshing sleep that did much to remedy the restless hours of the previous night. While she slept, Alan strolled by and Sandra smiled at him. He came over quietly and she indicated her friend.

'The Sleeping Beauty!' she hissed in a whisper, adding mischievously, 'To be awakened by a kiss from the prince?' To her utter dismay there was no answering smile in the stony eyes that now regarded her. She flushed and bit her lip. Both of them seemed to realise that any further attempts at light conversation would only exacerbate the situation, so Alan gave her a slight nod, made some lame excuse about the call of duty elsewhere, and walked off.

Fiona managed to doze for most of the morning and was surprised to find how much better she felt on awakening. The sunshine, happy chatter about her and the prospect of a conducted tour during the afternoon did much to revive her spirits.

Covertly she looked for Alan at lunchtime, but it appeared not to be one of the days he shared his meal with the passengers. She also hoped to catch a glimpse of him when disembarking for the excursion, but, other than screwing her head right round to look back at the ship—and thereby indicating to everyone else that she was desperately looking for someone—her sideways glances brought no sign of the tall figure of the captain.

The drive around the island was full of interest and both her friends made her feel welcome in their company. For a little while she was able to put Alan from her mind and gaily took snapshot after snapshot of everything that she thought would be of interest to look back upon during the dreary months of a cold winter at home. The people were gay and friendly, making no objection to being included in the photographs, while the children jostled each other to be the first in view. Small, laughing, olive-skinned pixies with dark hair who chattered away in Portuguese, sniggering and laughing because the three grown-ups could not understand what they said. As fast as Fiona lined them up, one would break free to run round to the other side, thereby causing his companions to wriggle with mirth. Finally Robert assumed a fierce expression, which drew further beams of delight, and wagged a long finger at the group. Fiona included him in two of her snaps.

'I shall frame them and hang them on the lounge wall

in our new home!' Sandra promised.

On their return to the ship, the purser called to Fiona as they walked past the office.

'A parcel has come for you, miss,' he said. 'I have it in my safe keeping.'

'A parcel? For me?' Fiona was mystified.

With a smile, the purser produced a tiny package and she thanked him, turning it over and over in her hands. Sandra also peered at it and winked.

'Have you a secret admirer on the island?' she suggested, noticing the perplexed frown on Fiona's face. She knew it would be safe to make a quip about the package because her friend had not recognised the handwriting. Had it been from someone like Alan, it might have been a different matter, where jokes were out of place at the present time.

'I wonder if it might be from Nancy,' Fiona murmured, 'because the handwriting is very old-fashioned and shaky. But why should she be sending *me* gifts? I only met her last night. And I'm certain I didn't leave anything behind at the house.'

'Then open it and put us both out of our misery!' Sandra begged as they walked towards their cabin. Inside, they had to use needlework scissors to split the layers of sticky tape sealing the paper.

'I should imagine Aenone wrapped it,' Sandra remarked as she sat on her bed, eager to see the parcel's contents. The brown paper fluttered to the floor and Fiona lifted off the lid of a small white box to reveal cotton wool. She removed the top layer and found a small piece of folded notepaper. Under it lay more cotton wool in the midst of which rested a delicate moonstone brooch set in filigree gold. Both girls gasped. Wordlessly, Fiona handed it to her friend, who turned it over and over.

'This is beautiful!' she exclaimed with delight.

'But why give it to me? You're the engaged girl; the one entitled to such gifts.'

'Read what she says, then we'll know.'

Slowly Fiona opened the note and read aloud:

'"My dear Fiona,

I would be so happy if you will accept this gift. It was given to me by a very dear friend, and thereby hangs quite a tale.

I feel it would be more fitting if you wore it for me.

Please visit the island again very soon and come and see me.

Yours affectionately,

Nancy."'

'Oh, do try it!' Sandra begged, leaping to her feet. 'Let me pin it for you. Not really suitable with the dress you're wearing, but we must see it on.'

Together they stared at Fiona's reflection in the mirror. She laid her hand over it gently and smiled.

'I wonder how she knew that moonstones were my favourite? It looks terribly expensive. Of course I can't accept it. I'll have to return it at once with a polite letter.'

'No, you can't.'

'But I have to! If I accept, she'll think I'm greedy, and out for what I can get. No, Sandra, I must write immediately.' She moved away from the mirror, unpinning the brooch as she went. Her friend's hand touched her arm and shook it.

'Just think for a moment before you embark on something you may regret later. Nancy is an old woman. Giving you this brooch probably means a very great deal to her.

If you send it back, she'll be terribly hurt and offended. Put yourself in her place. I don't suppose she gets all that much fun out of life, being tied to a wheelchair as she is. Her only enjoyment comes from the friends who find time to call. She met you last night, liked you, and felt she wanted to show you that she hopes the friendship may continue and deepen. And the only way she knew how, with the ship leaving in the morning, was to send you this lovely brooch which she, in turn, received long ago from a dear friend. I expect the friend's dead now, which is why she feels she can pass on the gift to someone like you. You should feel highly honoured that she already holds such a deep affection for you. No, Fiona, you certainly can't take the risk of offending her.'

'Nevertheless,' Fiona continued uncomfortably, 'I wish it had been you to whom she'd given the brooch. Gifts like this one are more suited to engaged girls.'

'Now we've got to find the right dress for you to wear this evening,' her friend remarked, flinging open the wardrobe door and beginning to rifle through the garments hanging there. 'Let me see, now ... nothing flowered, of course, or that will hide the brooch. Something really simple and plain ... ah, this blue one. We can pin the brooch slightly away from the neckline ... here.'

Fiona bent over a drawer in search of her writing case.

'I must make sure my thank-you letter goes ashore before we leave early in the morning. It would be dreadfully rude and casual to expect her to wait until I post a letter from home before thanking her. But, oh dear, what on earth can I say? I'm so overwhelmed by her generosity.'

'That's simple. Just tell her how much you appreciate such a gorgeous brooch and that you'll treasure it all your life. And thank her again for the lovely evening and say that you hope it won't be too long before you come back to Madeira to see her.'

'I only wish it could be a short time!' Fiona sighed wistfully. 'It'll take me years to save enough to pay for another holiday here, whether I come on a cruise again or fly over to stay on the island.'

'How about the good old legacy left by a doting uncle? Have you any?' Fiona laughed and shook her head. 'Or the football pools?'

'Neither do I indulge that way.'

'Then you'll just have to get married and bully your husband into bringing you here.'

'If I ever *do* get married, that is,' Fiona responded wistfully. 'No one in mind at the present, as well you know. Now, if you'll forgive me, I really must get on with this letter so it can be despatched ashore. Oh, aren't we both nitwits? We don't even know Nancy's address, although we know where to find her house.'

'Surely it's in her note?'

Fiona looked. 'No.'

'Then I'll ring Bob.' Sandra dialled and was soon through to his cabin where she explained her mission. She laughed. 'No, I'm not going to tell you just yet. You'll just have to wait and see, if you keep your eyes open. Fiona, pen and paper, please.' She waggled her fingers at the other girl, who promptly thrust the writing materials into her waiting hands. She scribbled in silence and then thanked him before ringing off.

Fiona found that it was not an easy letter to write. If the wording was too stilted, she would sound ungrateful; if too profuse, condescendingly effusive. Eventually she was satisfied with the few simple lines and signed her name with a sigh of relief.

'Now for the envelope and I'll take it straight along to the office for postage ashore.'

The first person to notice the brooch at dinner was Bob. Admittedly he had been warned to keep his eyes open and exaggeratedly gave both girls a thorough looking-over as they prepared to sit down.

'Well then,' he whispered to Sandra, 'what is it? I'd been building my hopes so high thinking that perhaps you'd both appear in something rather daring, like topless dresses . . .'

'Devil!' she hissed back fondly.

'Ah, I see. It's not you after all. 'Tis Fiona here with a very lovely brooch. Am I right?' The latter nodded, smiling. 'Nancy sent it, I presume. You're a very lucky girl. Treasure it well.'

'I shall, I promise.'

'Oh, my dears!' gushed Mrs Bottlin-Mabee from behind as she rushed up to the table. 'I'm very sorry to be late, but I very nearly didn't come at all. Hallo there, Doctor. Surprised to see me after all?' She twinkled archly at him as he rose to pull out her chair. 'I've really had a terribly disappointing day, you see. While all you other good people have been enjoying yourselves and making the most of your precious time, I've been languishing on a sickbed.' There were slight murmurs of sympathy as she looked round the table. 'I've consumed vast quantities of the dear doctor's dyspepsia tablets while lying in a darkened cabin. I'm absolutely positive I must have eaten something that was just that little bit tainted last night. I'm right, aren't I, Doctor?' She did not wait for dissent or agreement. 'But you were rather naughty, for you told me you didn't expect me to get up at all today, let alone join you all for dinner, and I've proved you wrong. When I saw that horrible invalid supper brought to me, I knew I was cured, and here I am. Naturally I wouldn't dream of indulging myself tonight, so I shall take the greatest care what I eat.'

Her greedy little eyes flashed about the table. 'Perhaps just a small portion of lobster?' She glanced towards Robert, who shook his head. She laughed. 'Ah well, perhaps that is expecting too much. Doctor must choose for me,' she declared magnanimously, and beamed at him. 'The truth is, I never, never over-indulge. It so happens that my stomach decides to have its little moments when it takes a ridiculous objection to some of the things that I *know* can't really hurt it. Oh, Fiona, I see you're wearing a new brooch. You haven't worn it before during the cruise, so I know it must be new. There isn't much I miss about the things worn by others of my sex!' she declared in triumph, feasting her eyes on the brooch and her nose almost beginning to twitch like a sniffing terrier's. 'Of course, it isn't real; anyone can see that. You wouldn't possibly have had enough holiday currency to buy such a thing here on Madeira if it were genuine. Nevertheless, don't think I'm trying to say it's been a bad buy, because I think it's absolutely lovely and only goes to show what wonderful things can be done with paste these days.'

Fiona had begun to flush hotly and Sandra was almost apoplectic with fury. She longed to clamp both hands over the bright, moving flash of vermilion that was the garrulous woman's mouth. She had a sharp retort ready on her lips when Robert stepped in to heal the breach.

'I agree, madam, miracles are wrought in this modern world by the manufacturers of plastics.' He shot a warm glance at Fiona, who smiled her thanks. They both knew that Mrs Bottlin-Mabee would now drop the subject because her own opinion had been confirmed, and she liked always to be right.

At that moment, Alan entered the dining-room and Mrs Bottlin-Mabee waved wildly to him, calling out: 'Captain! Captain!'

He came over and greeted everyone at the table.

'I'm sure you must be surprised to see me here tonight, because the doctor will have told you this morning that he'd been obliged to put me on his passenger sick list.'

'I'm pleased to see you've made a swift recovery, madam.'

'Oh, don't "madam" me!' she retorted coyly. 'Aren't we old enough friends to drop such formality? Anyway, I feel like my old self again, I'm happy to say.'

Alan's eyes idled towards Fiona's and there was warmth and tenderness in them. Her heart missed a beat. His glance travelled towards the brooch and he seemed to stiffen. The smile fled from his lips and his eyes glittered with ice. She stared back at him for a moment, then he excused himself and made for his own table.

Reluctantly her fingers closed over the brooch.

Whatever could be wrong now? she wondered, deeply disturbed.

When dinner was over, Sandra suggested they should all go and see the nightly film in the ship's cinema, but Fiona shook her head.

'If you two don't mind, I think I'll skip it tonight. I've a bit of a headache coming on, so I doubt if watching a film would do me any good.'

'Still a little under the weather from this morning?' Robert asked solicitously. 'Have you any aspirin, or would you like me to prescribe something else?'

'I shall be all right. As a matter of fact, I planned to

change my book while the library was reasonably empty.'

'Surely you haven't finished that one already?' Sandra protested. 'You only got it out the other day.'

'I'm bored with it.'

'Nurse that headache first, young woman,' Robert advised. 'Reading is just as bad as the cinema.'

'I know. I'll be careful, I promise. Enjoy the film.'

'We will. If not, we'll come and seek you out for a nice little natter,' Sandra replied.

It was true that there was the slight suspicion of a headache behind Fiona's eyes, but not sufficient to warrant any treatment. She was not in the mood for films and wanted to be alone to think about Alan. Why had he behaved so strangely at dinner? Covertly she had glanced towards his table and not once had he looked up to meet her gaze. If anything, he was deliberately looking away.

It was when she was on her way to change her book that Alan's steward came towards her.

'Miss Barclay, I have a message from the captain. If you could spare a few minutes, he'd like to see you in his day cabin, please.'

Fiona's heart skipped a beat. She swallowed hastily and nodded.

'Of course. Straight away.'

The steward accompanied her to Alan's quarters where he knocked on the door and announced Fiona, stepping aside to allow her to enter the day cabin. Alan looked up from the desk, his mouth set in a hard, forbidding line. He waved his right hand towards one of the armchairs.

'Please sit down.' His tone was icy. Fiona uttered a tiny, embarrassed laugh.

'What is all this?' she asked. 'I feel as if I were back at school again!'

He had risen from his chair at her entrance and now came slowly towards her, his very bulk emanating a strange menace which made her feel suddenly afraid. He ignored her remark, saying instead,

'Tell me, Fiona, why do you deliberately set out to taunt me? Does it give you a vicious satisfaction?'

She flushed angrily at his tone. 'I *beg* your pardon?'

'Don't pretend to misunderstand me, my love, because you know very well what I mean.' His right hand shot out and the tips of his fingers touched the brooch. 'This. Flaunting it before me in public.'

She tried to rise from her chair, but he pushed her back, leaning over her with both hands on the arms of the chair. His angry eyes were very close.

'I'm sure I don't know what you're getting at, Alan.'

'Then allow me to enlighten you. You wanted to provoke me, so you wore the brooch.'

'I did no such thing! I have no wish at all to ... to ... *provoke* you, as you say. In fact, all I can say is that you seem to have taken leave of your senses, talking in riddles.' She raised her hand to cover the brooch. 'Nancy gave me this brooch, and I shall treasure it greatly.' She paused when a sharp flash of pain crossed his face. He straightened at once and moved away so that she could no longer see his expression.

'When did she give it to you? At what stage last night was it handed over?'

'I fail to see why this concerns you!' Fiona retorted as her temper rose. 'I suppose you're jealous because Nancy wanted to give me a present even though we only met yesterday, while you're a friend of very long standing. I didn't realise men could be so petty! As you're so interested, and probably about to accuse me of avarice, I'll tell you that I didn't want to accept this expensive gift and was all for sending it back, but Sandra persuaded me not to. She said the giving of such a present gave Nancy much pleasure and it certainly wouldn't be right to hurt her by returning it.'

'I see.' He was toying with some papers on the desk, his back towards her. 'Why didn't you put it on straight away last night when she gave it to you, instead of waiting until this evening?'

'For the very simple reason that I only received it to-night. It was brought down to the ship. I hope that satis-fies your curiosity? And, if that's all you wanted me for, I'd like to leave now, please.'

He spun round, his face dark with fury and passion. 'No, it most certainly is *not* all! When you and Nancy were alone together, having your heart-to-heart last night, did you beg her to find some means of winning me back, is that what happened?'

Fiona almost choked on her anger and her cheeks burned. She swallowed hard in an effort to maintain control. 'Alan, I'm doing my very best to remain charitable towards you, although you seem determined to be as rude and offensive as possible. All I can say is that obviously you're under stress and feeling the strains of command. Perhaps it would be wiser if Robert were to prescribe a strong sedative so you can get some sleep. Nancy was right, you're overtired. Maybe you'll feel better in the morning. I sincerely hope so, for everyone's sake. This whole interview has mystified me. All this fuss about a very charming brooch given me by a dear, sweet old lady! I fail to see why you should concern yourself with the whys and wherefores of my pre-sent. Or do you probe into the private affairs of every passenger?' she finished bitterly.

He studied her, a thoughtful frown marring his brow. 'Do you mean you really don't know?'

'Haven't I just said so?'

'The truth behind the brooch?'

'As I've patiently tried to explain but you don't seem able to understand, Nancy wanted to give me a present and chose this brooch. It isn't new, if that's what's bothering you so much. She said in her note that it was given her by a very dear friend and . . . oh, no!' Her voice tailed off and her mouth dropped open in horror as realisation dawned. In a whisper, she continued: 'Did you give it to her? Are you that dear friend?'

'Yes.'

Fiona bit her lip. 'I understand now. No wonder you were rather annoyed. I'm terribly sorry, Alan. I won't wear it again if it angers you. Nancy should have explained, although her note said there was a story behind the brooch.'

'There is indeed,' Alan agreed with vehemence. 'I suppose now we've gone so far, I'd better tell you the rest.' He came close to her, reaching down again to touch the brooch. He turned it gently, the pin straining at the soft fabric of her dress. 'I suppose it's rather sad, really. I bought this a few years ago, intending it for you.' He heard the slight gasp of her indrawn breath. 'Yes, my love. It was to be a rather special wedding present from your loving husband-to-be.'

'No!' Her hand flew up to close over the brooch, her fingers just missing contact with his as he drew sharply back. 'Nancy was naughty. She should have explained.'

'I knew how much you loved moonstones. When you refused even to explain why you no longer wanted to marry me, I almost threw this into the sea. I could have taken it back to the jewellers, then I thought of the second woman

I loved—Nancy. I knew she would be curious as to why I was giving her such an expensive gift, so I told her everything.'

Fiona hung her head, tears very close.

'So, my dear, if she didn't explain its history, why do you suppose she gave it to you?'

She did not respond.

'When you wore this tonight, I immediately presumed you'd done so to taunt me. I almost struck you as you sat, smiling, at the dinner table. Now I see how very mistaken I've been. And I must ask you to forgive me for the harsh accusations I made, although I think you'll agree that everything looked very black.' He paused, seeing her nod her head. 'Very well, we have to ask ourselves why Nancy chose this moment to give you the brooch I'd bought for you.'

'Perhaps ... perhaps she thought it might bring us together again?' Fiona suggested after a very long pause.

'Perhaps, indeed. But she didn't know the terms under which I had agreed to have you, did she?' Another long pause. 'Very well, what are we going to do about it? Doubtless Nancy will be expecting some reaction from the gift. Awaiting eagerly for news, so what am I to tell her? Unfortunately Nancy has romantic notions about today's world when in reality it's harsh and uncompromising. She would like us to let bygones be bygones and for me to ask you to marry me. I'm sorry, I have to disappoint her, I'm afraid. Marriage is out of the question, as well you know.'

Nancy's words boomed through Fiona's head ... try him and see what happens ... see what happens ...

'I know. I haven't forgotten,' she whispered. 'Is your—your other offer still open?' She looked up and saw his eyes narrow while a strained alertness seemed to invade his body. 'You said ... about me ... you remember.'

Slowly he reached down for her hand and drew her to a standing position. He clasped her shoulders and felt her wince.

'You mean you're willing to become my mistress?' He raised her chin with forefinger and thumb, then began an unnerving caressing of her skin. 'Not just for now but for as long as I want you? Until I tire of you and cast you aside in favour possibly of someone else?'

The brutal words cut like a whip, but somehow she managed to nod.

'I see.' He moved away and began to pace the cabin floor, finally halting once again before her.

'You're asking me to make love to you?' She closed her eyes briefly and then reopened them. 'I want you, Fiona. I want you desperately. Are you still absolutely certain you want to come to me under my terms?'

Once again she closed her eyes and missed seeing the sudden light in his.

'Yes, Alan, I am,' came the whispered response.

'Very well.' He paused and a strange smile illuminated his eyes. 'There's no time like the present,' he continued in an unpleasantly matter-of-fact tone. Almost as if he had been ordering a change of course, Fiona thought. Her gaze was drawn to him and she watched, nearly mesmerised. One by one the buttons of his shirt were unfastened, then he tugged its tail free. His naked chest loomed before her as his arms reached for her. His fingers sought her dress zip and pulled it down. His face drew nearer and his lips began to part her own. She was shaking with fright, but she steeled herself to remain passive. After all, she told herself wildly, only the first time will be bad. When I'm a fallen woman, I shall find it so much easier.

His hands were evoking hitherto unknown feelings within her. She turned her head to return kiss for kiss and flung her arms about his waist, forcing herself to stroke the taut skin of his back. She moaned softly in her throat and clung to him, matching the pressure of his body with her own. He pulled away his mouth to kiss her throat and she cried:

'Oh, Alan, I love you so much!'

It was as if her words had broken a spell. He snatched away his lips, pushed both hands into her hips and thrust her away from him. There were beads of perspiration along his upper lip and a strange fire blazing in his eyes. She stared back at him. He spun her round and rezipped her dress. Then he strode to the cabin door and flung it open.

'Go, woman. For God's sake, go!'

And she went, scurrying down the corridor as if pursued by devils. Once within the sanctuary of her own cabin, she flung herself down on the bed and wept bitterly.

What had gone wrong just now? Alan had started to make love to her and she had responded fervently, so why had he then spurned her? And, most important of all, was she really sorry?

She rolled over on to her back and stared up at the ceiling through misted eyes. If she took herself to task, and really studied the question, she must now admit to being relieved he had thrust her from him. Had he continued making love to her, she would have fully acquiesced. Later she would begin to regret bitterly. Alan had put her to the test and she had found herself wanting. It had been proved to her now that never again would she be able to bring herself to offer Alan her body so blatantly. It did not matter how much she loved him; she simply could not surrender her principles.

And it was horribly, horribly true. She loved him with all her heart and soul.

Becoming his mistress was definitely not the way for her. She had to be his wife, or nothing.

Nancy was wrong. Fiona had now seen what would happen if she had given in to Alan. Perhaps Nancy had meant her to discover this truth? Was that the reason for her suggesting it be put to the test? That Fiona must learn she was a girl of decent principles. For her, love did not mean the casual surrender of her body to the man for whom she yearned. Marriage was the only answer. If there was to be no marriage, then there could not be anything else between them.

At least the problem had been resolved. Had Nancy known the answer, yet urged Fiona to discover it for herself so that now she could face life surely and squarely, and without doubts? In time, perhaps, peace of mind would become Fiona's again and she would have nothing to look back upon with bitterness or shame. Just regret at losing Alan the day she had jilted him.

It was too late to turn back the clock. The voyage would soon be over and they would go their separate ways.

At least I have this to remember Alan by, Fiona consoled herself, her fingers caressing the moonstone brooch.

By the time Sandra returned to the cabin, Fiona had regained her self-control and there were no traces whatsoever of the tears with which she had been blinded. And now she was able to say very truthfully that she had a slight headache.

And heartache. But that was her own private secret.

The cruise ship left the island in the early hours of the following morning. Not many of the passengers were awake to witness this departure, most being firmly tucked in their beds. Fiona had spent another restless night when all her thoughts were full of Alan, so she was glad of the opportunity to get up betimes and creep quietly from the cabin to watch the departure on deck.

Let the time pass quickly! she thought. Let the remaining days fly past, and let me not see him too often.

The ship was well under way and Fiona watched until the fast-diminishing houses blended into the landscape and soon the island was dipping over the horizon. She wondered whether Nancy had awakened early and was now lying in bed smiling at her success with the brooch.

Poor Nancy! She had meant well, but it was a mistake.

The brooch now nestled in its tiny box, where it would remain until Fiona had reached home again. She would not take it out during the rest of the cruise. Knowing all it had meant to Alan, she certainly could not bring herself to flaunt it before him a second time. Later, when she was home, and no one knew the brooch's history, she would wear it every day. And treasure it carefully. It would become part of her, and act as a physical reminder of her own stupidity. It would bring pain, just as being away from Alan must hurt her, yet she could overcome this. In time. Oh, yes, in a very, very long time ...

The gulls wheeled and turned over the ship and Fiona's eyes grew misty. She knew where Alan must be at this moment. On the bridge, in command of his vessel. She dared not even show interest in that direction. If she turned, if she looked up there, and caught his eye ...

She blinked quickly. From now on the sight of his tall figure could cause her nothing but acute pain.

If only the cruise were over tomorrow!

CHAPTER SEVEN

THROUGHOUT most of that day the passengers' conversations centred around Madeira and all they had seen and done while visiting the island. Fiona nodded and smiled with the best of them, although her heart was not with the chatter. She felt considerably relieved when she allowed herself to be dragged away by an eager Tommy for a game of deck quoits. He was surprisingly nimble on his feet for his diminutive size and kept her dashing all around the court. Whenever she missed one of his cunning throws, he shrieked with laughter, and many of the passengers stopped to watch and share the enjoyment. Finally Fiona was obliged to beg a halt.

'Please,' she panted, 'can't we stop for just one moment? I have a horrible stitch in my side.'

'But I'm winning! You can't stop now because it wouldn't be fair. In any case,' he lowered his voice and swivelled his eyes to the right, 'the captain's coming and I want him to see how much I've improved.'

Involuntarily, Fiona glanced towards Alan and met his sardonic gaze. The corners of his mouth were twitching and she wondered furiously whether he was amused at her dishevelled hair and fiercely red face caused by all the rushing about. He gave her the briefest of nods, smiled broadly at Tommy, and then walked on.

'Captain! Captain!' Tommy called after him. Alan paused and turned round. 'I'm winning, you know. I've got her just where I want her.'

Alan's eyebrows rose and he grinned at Fiona's obvious discomfort.

'Indeed? Lucky boy. Carry on and win by a wide margin.'

'I shall, you just wait and see. I'll beat Fiona into the ground. Ready?' And, without waiting for his opponent's reply, he flung the quoit wildly out of court.

'My point this time, I think,' Fiona said with satisfaction.

'I was only practising. We'll start properly now.'

'No. You asked whether I was ready ...'

'And you weren't, so it can't be a point. That's right, isn't it, Captain Howard?' Tommy turned to Alan for confirmation, but he was no longer there. The boy's face fell. 'Oh! He didn't even stay to watch. He usually does.'

'Perhaps he has work to do. A captain's life isn't all watching what his passengers get up to, you know,' Fiona remarked. 'He has a ship to run.'

'Pooh! That's easy. What are the crew for? The captain just sits up there on that bridge thing, or else reads books in his cabin while every one else does the work. I know, because I've seen it all in the films on telly. Now are you ready? Catch!'

The day passed surprisingly swiftly for Fiona and it was time to dress for dinner.

'Aren't you going to wear your new brooch?' Sandra asked as Fiona chose a flowered dress on which any other ornament would have been superfluous. 'Do come here and look at this,' she added, peering closely at a tiny blemish on her skin. 'Is that a spot coming, do you think? I hope not, because I hate spots.'

Fiona studied the mark and shook her head.

'Imagination, that's all.'

'Sure?'

'Yes.'

'Good. Spots were the scourge of my adolescence so I'm always wary if another appears, just in case I have a spate of them. That's good, isn't it? A spate of spots. Rather like a gaggle of geese!'

When dinner started, the captain's place at his table was still empty and Fiona watched it covertly, wondering if he were going to dine with the passengers tonight or in the privacy of his cabin. Alan arrived less than five minutes later and strode quickly through the restaurant to take his seat. He was immaculately dressed as usual and looked so handsome that Fiona almost cried out with the pain of longing. He glanced briefly towards her, included her in the briefest of nods he gave the assembly and then sat down amid a babble of talk from those at the table. Fiona kept her eyes averted from that table throughout the meal and assumed a gaiety she certainly did not feel.

Towards the end of dinner, there was a diversion as Alan rose to his feet and banged on the table for silence.

'Ladies and gentlemen, friends,' he began, 'tonight is another of those very special occasions we all like to celebrate together.'

'A birthday again!' Fiona's neighbour hissed in her ear. 'There you are, you see? The chef's procession with the cake. And *what* a cake!'

All eyes were fixed on the door leading from the kitchen as the iced cake was carried triumphantly into the room, held high for everyone to see. The chef paused in the centre, eager to discover the identity of the recipient. Alan smiled and beckoned towards his own table. There was a murmur of anticipatory conversation as people speculated as to whom would be honoured by tonight's favour. A space was cleared and the big cake deposited while the occupants of the table began demanding eagerly of one another in excited tones:

'Is it you? You never said—'

'You, maybe? Sly dog!'

Alan again pressed for silence while the chef's procession waited quietly behind the table.

'Ladies and gentlemen, I am even more delighted to tell you that this is no birthday celebration as you all seem to presume. It is in the way of being ... er ... let me put it this way ...' he seemed confused, Fiona thought, '... yes, a double occasion for celebration. I'm sure you will want to join me and my crew,' he paused momentarily as the duty officer who had been striding quickly towards his table reached him. 'Excuse me, please. Yes, what is it?' he demanded in a lowered voice. The officer handed him a folded piece of paper which Alan opened, perused swiftly, and then slid into a pocket. He nodded and the officer turned to leave.

'I beg your pardon for that slight interruption, ladies and gentlemen, when I know you're all on tenterhooks to learn what we are about to celebrate tonight. I'm sure you will want to join me and the crew in wishing every happiness for their future married life together to our good friend and, to some not quite so hardy as others, our comforter, Doctor Robert Maynard, and his fiancée Mrs Sandra Stern. Chef, the doctor's table, please.' Alan smiled at Robert amid a chorus of exclamation while the chef picked up the cake again to carry it to Robert's table. Hastily Fiona and her neighbour pushed aside plates and glasses to make room.

'You sly old things!' she whispered to Sandra. 'Not even a whisper to me. I thought you were going to wait until you reached home?'

Under the storm of clapping, Sandra replied happily, 'We were, but Robert changed his mind this morning. However, I never expected it to be made public like this. I'm just as flabbergasted as you, believe me. I see Robert knew all about it!' she smiled accusingly into her fiancé's red face and he beamed back at her before her attention was drawn to another diner, eager to congratulate her. Robert's eyes swivelled towards Alan's table and he frowned, saying almost to himself,

'That's odd. There was more to come, but he's leaving.'

Fiona's gaze followed Alan's hasty departure until someone addressed her and she forgot about him.

It took some time for the excitement to die down, then together Sandra and Robert cut the first slice of cake before they laughingly relinquished the task to the expert hands of the chef, who then deftly divided the masterly creation into shared portions.

'When are you planning to marry?' someone was asking behind Fiona, while another demanded to know whether Sandra would live aboard so that she might accompany Robert on future cruises.

'Perhaps you'll want to leave the sea and settle ashore?' a third person suggested.

'I don't know what our future plans will be,' Sandra replied to all the persistent questions. 'We really haven't had time yet to make any decisions.'

Fiona's eyes were on the door and her heart thudded when Alan reappeared. He looked worried as he wound his way between the tables and the crowd gathered around Robert's to reach his own. Once there, he banged heftily for silence. Everyone turned to look at him.

'Ladies and gentlemen, I am sorry to have to interrupt this happy occasion, but I've just received news which I feel it's my duty to pass on to you all. I shall also be seeking any help you feel you can give. Perhaps a few of you may have noticed that we've altered course and are now sailing at full speed. We've received an urgent message to go to the aid of a stricken Greek cruise liner which has suffered an explosion in her boiler room and is unable to proceed. No,' he raised one hand to stem the excited buzz of speculation, 'fortunately there are few casualties, but immediate assistance is required to take on her complement of about two hundred passengers.'

'Two *hundred?*'

'But where will you put them all?'

'We're the only vessel in the immediate vicinity and should reach the liner's position shortly before dawn tomorrow. Accommodation, however, poses a problem. There are still a few unused cabins while many of you have vacant berths in shared cabins. Should anyone feel inclined to offer to double up with someone else ... ladies with ladies, gentlemen with gentlemen, I'm afraid,' he added to much laughter, 'then we shall be only too pleased to know. The purser will take all offers of help in his office. We expect to have to take one of the public rooms out of service for use as a dormitory for the other passengers, but notification will be posted as soon as possible outside the purser's office. I must also ask you all, should you wish to witness the transfer of passengers from the crippled liner, to obey the ship's officers and not step into the areas which will be designated after we have arrived. Thank you. Please continue to enjoy yourselves.' He looked pointedly towards Robert's table, but the doctor was already pushing his way towards him. The two men left the room, deep in discussion.

'I know one thing, and that's for sure,' Mrs Bottlin-

Mabee declared loudly, 'I'm not sharing my cabin with anyone from another ship. The very nerve of it, I must say! Having paid all this money to come on a cruise and then to be told to "double up".'

Fiona turned the full power of her eyes upon the selfish woman.

'It's only right to offer whatever help we can.'

'That's the prerogative of youth, my dear. When you've lived as long as I have ... which isn't *that* long, actually ... you learn to be choosey. I like my cabin to myself. I cannot abide someone snoring in the next bed. In any case, my dear, we've all paid good money for this cruise and shouldn't be expected to give something up halfway. No, I shall write to the Managing Director of the line to complain about Captain Howard's high-handed attitude in *presuming* passengers are prepared to assist.'

'Mrs Bottlin-Mabee, may I remind you that it's one of the unwritten laws of the sea to go to the aid of anyone in distress?'

'Huh!'

'Would you still be so derogatory if it was this vessel now wallowing about without power? I doubt it. You'd be eager for any helping hand held out to you.'

'That's different, you silly girl. We are now obliged to be invaded by hordes of people we don't know ... and probably won't like, because they'll all be Greek ... and have to share the tables and everything with them. I shall demand my money back, that I will.'

'Yes, Mrs Bottlin-Mabee,' Sandra intervened, her voice cold and calm in spite of the heat of her anger, 'you do so, and I hope you get great satisfaction from your action. Come on, Fiona, let's see what help we can offer.' She tugged her friend away from the table and pulled a wry face. 'I could *hit* that overfed, horrible face sometimes! Let's hope she keeps to her cabin and stays well out of our way for the rest of the voyage. I'm going to find Robert. I want to help in sick bay. How about you?'

'Alan said there were few casualties, but I wonder exactly what he meant by "a few"? Perhaps he didn't want to alarm us.'

'Robert will know.'

When they approached Robert's tiny office in the hospital unit, the nurse emerged, speaking over her shoulder as she came.

'I'll see to it at once, sir. Oh,' she paused to address Sandra, 'Mrs Stern, is anything wrong? You're not sick, I hope?'

'No. We wanted a word with Robert if he isn't too busy,' Sandra replied, while Fiona hung back a little. 'Is he in the office?'

'Yes, but the captain's with him.'

Fiona tugged at her friend's arm.

'We can come back later when he isn't so busy,' she suggested, but Robert's voice called out to them to enter the office. He came over to Sandra and gripped her hand.

'Darling, this is nice. Missing me already?' he teased.

Alan stood behind the desk, a sheet of paper in his hand. He gave Fiona a brief smile and continued to read.

'Yes, I am missing you. Darling, we've decided we must help you, if you'll let us. I'm sure you're going to be frantically busy down here. Before you say no, let me reassure you that we don't want to interfere in anything medical. But there'll be plenty of other things to do like cleaning, the dishes, beds to be made, books to be fetched for the patients and countless other things which I'm sure Nurse will be far too occupied to attend to herself. May we help, please?'

Alan answered for Robert.

'Although I didn't say much in public, we expect to be overflowing down here. It's very good of you two, if you're sure you really want to give up your free time? It won't be just for one day, you realise?'

'We've thought it all out. And we've also decided on something else, too. If we pack everything we don't need and just keep out the bare essentials for the rest of the voyage home, could our suitcases be stored somewhere? And we're willing to be squeezed into a tiny space so that two other people may have the use of our cabin.'

'We've been discussing the knotty problem of accommodation,' Robert replied quickly. 'I'm expecting some of the Greek medical staff to join me here and only the injured crew members. The rest of the officers and men remain aboard until the tug arrives to tow them into the nearest suitable port. Alan is planning to move in with the First Officer, although he must still retain the use of his day cabin. This is the answer to your question, Alan. The girls can share it, and then you have the advantage at least of knowing who your two squatters are! Almost like having a pedigree. Also,' he winked at Sandra and then smiled mischievously in Fiona's direction, 'it's such a waste of a large bed if you don't fill it properly. You've often complained that there was room enough for two, but then it was designed mainly for married captains.'

Fiona's cheeks burned and she could not bring herself even to glance at Alan, who muttered under his breath:

'Quite so.'

'We won't intrude upon your work in the day cabin,' Sandra promised. 'We'll come and go like two little mice, but I expect we shall be so busy down here with Robert that you'll hardly know we're about. And too tired after duty hours to do anything but sleep!'

Fiona was not so sure she favoured the idea of being so close to Alan—with only a thin bulkhead separating them. She knew she would be tense, wondering what he was doing while she lay waiting for sleep. She had envisaged a small linen cupboard or store somewhere, with hammocks slung between shelves perhaps, or maybe sleeping bags spread out upon the floor for them. But never Alan's bed! And not so soon after her attempt to ... to ... but she wouldn't think of that now.

She shook her head to rid it of the treacherous thoughts.

'I regret that Mrs Bõttlin-Mabee is not prepared to surrender her privacy,' Sandra announced out of the blue. Robert's eyebrows quirked.

'Indeed? And she has a spare bunk.'

'She threatens to complain to the Managing Director.'

'That's her privilege.' Alan remarked without raising his head from the paper he was studying. 'However, it may become necessary either to move her out, or someone else in. We'll just have to wait and see how things go. I was hoping to obtain private accommodation for the women and children, if not the men.'

'Shall we go and start packing?' Sandra demanded. 'Would you like us out of the cabin before morning?'

'Yes, that would indeed be helpful.'

'If the stewardess brings fresh linen, we could remake the beds for her. I'm sure she'll have a great deal to attend to without unnecessary work for us.'

Alan smiled his thanks and replaced the paper on the desk. He came over to Sandra and squeezed her arm gently.

'I wish all my passengers were like you two.'

'Now that indeed *is* a compliment from a normally crusty old bachelor!' Robert teased gaily. 'Although, had the

Duty Officer timed his appearance with a little more finesse, he might . . .' He was not allowed to finish as Alan turned on him, his expression dark with anger and voice harsh.

'That's enough, Robert! There isn't time for levity, and sometimes you carry a joke just that little too far. Now, girls, if you'll forgive me, I have much to do and a great deal on my mind. I'll speak to my steward and he'll have my night cabin ready for you within the hour. My first task is to see how much success the purser has had.'

'Not a great deal, I'm afraid,' Sandra replied sadly. 'At least, there was hardly anyone waiting to speak to him when we passed.'

'I didn't expect one mad rush, because folks tend to change their minds after the first flush of enthusiasm. I prefer them to have time to think things over and then they're likely to be more sincere in their offers. Also, when dawn comes and finds us alongside the Greek ship, the hesitant may experience a change of heart. I'll see you both later. A cup of coffee, perhaps, in my day cabin before you turn in? You, too, Robert, if you're free?'

'Thank you. I'll see what I can do.'

'You'll be there, I know. You have a fiancée to kiss good-night.' And, with that unexpectedly cheerful remark, Alan smiled warmly and then left them, striding away with a purposeful tread.

It was a subdued gathering of passengers that lined the rail early the next morning to watch the transfer from the stricken Greek cruise vessel. Somehow, no one felt excitement; this was a solemn occasion, in which many things might go wrong. The sea condition bordered on the unfavourable, with a heavy swell. This meant that the two parent ships must lie some distance apart as all engines were stopped. The thin light of dawn shed an uncanny hue over the proceedings until the sun rose abruptly over the horizon.

It could not have been pleasant, Fiona thought as the ship rolled sluggishly beneath her feet. Lying hove-to at the mercy of the sea's motion must have tried even the toughest stomach. Some of the onlookers had begun to slip away, seeking solace with their seasickness remedies, and even she was not sure she would want any breakfast.

The journey in the lifeboats must have been a nightmare. The tiny vessels rose and fell as they ploughed their way across the intervening strip of ocean. Many of the passengers were grey-faced when they were helped aboard the rescue ship, and most of the children had begun to cry fretfully.

'We'd better go down,' Sandra advised at Fiona's side. 'I'm sure the injured have been brought over in those boats that made for our stern. Robert will be needing us.'

The sick bay seethed with activity as people bustled about. The two girls stood aside as a stretcher was carried past. An elderly woman lay on it with her eyes closed and her right hand clasped tightly in her husband's.

'What's wrong with her, I wonder?' Sandra whispered in her companion's ear.

The stretcher-bearers were directed to a bed at the far end of the ward and curtains pulled around it.

'What may we do?' Fiona asked as the nurse hurried past.

'I think cups of tea are the order of the day,' she smiled back. 'To counter the effects of the unpleasant transfer.'

It was not until much later that Fiona learned why the elderly woman passenger had been brought for treatment.

She had suffered a slight heart attack shortly after the explosion, which had not been helped by the bumpy trip across in the lifeboat, and Robert felt a constant eye should be kept on her for the next twenty-four hours.

Fiona was so busy that she did not realise the rolling had ceased and that once again they were under way. She had been delegated the task of helping an injured seaman with thickly bandaged hands drink from a feeder cup. He must have been in some pain, although he did his utmost to hide this while she was with him, even going so far as to quip her at length in Greek, none of which she was able to understand.

'I'm sorry, but I really don't know what you're saying,' she told him, and then repeated it in excruciating French. Still he grinned at her and shook his head. From the adjacent bed a hand prodded her back and she turned round.

'I speak ... just English some little. Takis say ... if you sweet like the tea drinking, then make a date with you when renewed.'

Fiona laughed. 'When he's better, you mean.' She smiled down at her patient. 'More tea?' He continued to beam at her and she turned to his companion. 'Could you please ask Takis if he would like another cup of tea?' The man did so, and Takis nodded vigorously. She fetched it from the trolley in the centre of the ward and proceeded to help him drink again.

'Takis only drink second because you stay with him, he like.'

'Oh,' Fiona swiftly translated the statement, 'you mean he only wants it to keep me with him?'

'Yes. Yes. So.'

'Then please tell him I have much work to do,' Fiona demonstrated with her free hand, 'and I cannot give all my time to just one person.'

'Sad. He disappoint badly.'

'But I shall come back later.'

When the feeder cup had been emptied for the second time, Fiona collected all the other cups and stacked them on the trolley before wheeling it out of the ward. She pulled up sharply as she almost collided with a tall figure who was emerging from a treatment room.

'Careful, please, the plaster's still wet,' Alan said, and then added: 'Oh, it's you.' He paused, while the small girl in his arms sniffed loudly and stared at Fiona. 'Can you leave that for one moment and steady the foot while I carry her to bed?'

'Of course.' Fiona parked her trolley close to the wall and placed one hand under the wet whiteness of the child's foot. 'Hallo,' she said, smiling into the woebegone face.

'Heidi is German and unable to understand much English. I know you don't understand her language, but she knows the meaning of "hallo" all right. At the moment she's feeling rather miserable with this painful leg. Isn't that so, pet?' He smiled into Heidi's face and she responded by tightening her arms about his neck. Fiona felt strangely cut off from them both. She swallowed and asked:

'What happened? I thought you had said there were few casualties amongst the passengers?'

'Unfortunately she tripped while getting into the lifeboat and Robert now says she has a greenstick fracture of the ankle. It should mend very quickly because she's young, and greensticks are not complete breaks. In the meantime, Robert has condemned her to this horrible plaster cast. This way, Fiona. I'm to put her in one of the single rooms where her mother is waiting.'

A small, delicately-boned woman rose from the chair

where she had been sitting and smiled at her daughter, who promptly burst into tears. Alan spoke rapidly in German.

'She's perfectly all right now, just a little scared. The doctor wants her to rest in bed until the plaster has dried, then she can return to a more normal way of life. Nurse will be in in a moment to explain how the leg must be rested.'

'Thank you, Captain. Now, Heidi, stop crying and say thank you to the kind captain for helping you.' She tucked her daughter's hand into her own and the sobbing ceased. Her eyes flashed towards Fiona, who smiled back.

'Miss Barclay will be here to fetch anything you need,' Alan continued. 'You will find her extremely helpful.' In English, he added:

'I think we should leave them together now, Fiona. Come along.' Meekly she obeyed. When they were outside the ward, Alan sighed and she suddenly realised how tired he must be feeling.

'Would you like a cup of tea? I'm sure I can rustle you up a cup.'

'I'd love one, but I really can't stay. I shouldn't have been here in the first place, but Heidi was in such distress that ... well, you know.' He smiled wryly and gave her a good-natured shrug. 'Never could resist kids, I suppose. Managing all right between you?'

'I think so. At least, neither Robert nor Nurse have complained of Sandra and me getting in their way.'

'I must go and see how my officers are coping with this invasion. And plan my next move.'

'Which port will we ... oh, my goodness, look who's coming now!' Fiona's enquiring tone turned to one of dismay as Mrs Bottlin-Mabee rounded the corner and bore purposefully down on them. Alan sighed.

'I've just remembered something I want to discuss with Robert, but it seems I'm not quick enough to avoid the coming confrontation,' he murmured in a low voice. Mrs Bottlin-Mabee waved an arm at him and called out.

'Cooee, Captain! Captain Howard, now don't go away, because I've been hunting all over the boat for you. No one else wants to hear what I have to say and the purser says he's far too busy at the moment dealing with all the other riff-raff. Hallo, dear, how are you getting on with your Florence Nightingale bit? Silly child to be so quixotic! Still, he's engaged to your friend, so there's no real point in continuing to pursue him, is there?'

'I beg your pardon!' Fiona was deeply affronted and flushed. Alan moved to her side and, surreptitiously, gave her hand a quick squeeze.

'And what may I ...' he began, but Mrs Bottlin-Mabee forestalled him by blurting out,

'At times I can be rather rash in my words, Captain,' she gushed, and laid a podgy hand on his arm, 'but of course you must all know I don't really mean all I say in the heat of the moment. Admittedly I was very angry last night at being turned so rudely out of my cabin. It certainly wasn't right, you know, and I can't forgive you fully, you understand. I shall still be writing to the Managing Director, whatever you say or do for me from now on. However, the letter need not be quite so harsh if you'll do as I say. I thought it an insult to be turned out of my very comfortable cabin and made to bed down with that poky-nosed little frump, Miss Munroe. Of course it wasn't easy to say too much last night, with everyone coming and going as if the whole place was on fire, and really we were only getting ready for some hundreds of other people to flock aboard and take away all our own amenities. That, of course, I shall tell the Managing Director when I enumerate my various reasons for a full refund of cash. I only wish I knew him personally, but he isn't on the long list of my late, dear husband's business associates, more's the pity. I didn't want to share quarters, but I do now. But not with that Miss Munroe who does nothing but complain because I need more drawer space than she's willing to let me have.'

'Please come to the point, Mrs Bottlin-Mabee,' Alan interrupted, with a very pointed glance at his watch. 'I'm an exceedingly busy man.'

'Not too busy to ignore the comfort and wishes of every single passenger, I trust?' the other woman smirked, and batted her eyelids at Alan. 'However, what I really wanted to say was that you'd never believe my luck. It's incredible how well some things happen, just when you're expecting only the very worst.' She turned a reptilian smile upon Fiona who stood quietly in the background. 'I don't know why you're here listening to all this, dear, because it should have been private between myself and the captain. Nevertheless, I can't be cross with you, because I'm so terribly happy everything's turned out in my favour. In any case, the captain can give you the order to take back to the purser, so you might as well stay here until I've told him the rest of my good news. There I was, standing where I could have a good look at all those strange foreigners coming aboard, when I spotted her. You could have knocked me down with a boathook, or whatever it is you nautical folk say! We just stared at each other to start with, as if we couldn't believe our eyes. Then I smiled and she smiled and I shouted her name and then we were hugging and kissing each other. Wasn't it wonderful?'

'You mean, one of the passengers on the Greek ship is

a relative?' Alan asked.

'Oh no, nothing like that. I thought you realised there aren't many of us left now. I'm the last. No, Captain, she and I met a few years ago on a similar cruise to this, then we lost touch. I don't know why, because we both promised faithfully to write. Perhaps she changed her address and forgot to notify me; I'll ask her later, but there's so much else to talk about. She really was terribly silly, because she could have written to me instead of flying all that way over from America to join her ship in Greece, and then we could have come together on this cruise. Now there isn't much time left, but we'll make the best of it. So will you write a note to the purser, please, Captain? We discussed the relative merits of our cabins and I've decided that the one she's sharing is much better than Miss Munroe's, so I'll move out of that one and the woman in with my friend can go to Miss Munroe's. Then everyone will be happy. I'm sure there must be plenty of paper and a pen in the doctor's office, so if you'll write the order now, I'll take it to the purser. And you, dear,' she now addressed Fiona, 'can come along and help carry my baggage. I'm not supposed to carry very heavy things because they make me breathless, so while there are young limbs available, I shall make use of them. Are you going to write, Captain?'

'Certainly, Mrs Bottlin-Mabee. If you're sure that's the way you want it?'

'Haven't I just explained?'

'Yes, madam, but I simply wish to point out that this must be your final change of mind where accommodation is concerned.'

Mrs Bottlin-Mabee took immediate offence and drew herself up to address him in cold, condescending tones.

'My dear Captain Howard, may I remind you that it

was *your* wish ... nay, your direct *order* ... in the first place for your regular passengers to be uprooted against their wills. I consider your remark to be most ungenerous and exceedingly discourteous, but I shall put it down to exhaustion on your part, coupled with the frank inability to cope successfully with the present situation. I am an old and good client of this shipping line, so I'm sure all my complaints will be viewed with the utmost care at Head Office. I've often believed that those who sit behind desks in busy towns are not always the wisest of judges when it comes to selecting men to captain their big liners. Naturally I shall inform the Managing Director of my opinion when I write a full and competent report of everything that has happened during the past twenty-four hours. I shall even request an interview with him so that I may express my displeasure in person. What have you to say to that, eh?' she finished in triumph.

Fiona glanced swiftly from one to the other and crossed her fingers behind her back.

'To complain is your privilege, madam,' came Alan's gentle response. 'I must bide my time until I, too, am summoned to answer for my actions. In the meantime, however, I shall continue to run this ship and to issue such orders as *I* see fit. If you'll excuse me, I have that note to write.'

'Young man, kindly do not turn your back on me until I've finished! I have one more matter to discuss with you, and that's the problem of places in the restaurant. I understand from my stewardess ... who, incidentally, seemed rather vague and hazy about the whole thing ... that our extra passengers will be expected to dine at a later sitting. Now this frankly will not do, because Lettice and I shall be dining together at the doctor's table. Space must be found for her, so I suggest you send that young Tommy to the nursery.'

'Your friend may certainly sit at the table with you,' came the surprising reply, 'and Tommy will remain with his parents, or beside his young friend at the other table, should he so wish. There'll be a place vacant in any case because the doctor is to take most of his meals in the hospital, likewise Miss Barclay and Mrs Stern.'

'Oh, I see.' Mrs Bottlin-Mabee was considerably deflated. 'Then that's settled. The note, if you please.'

Without another word, Alan disappeared into Robert's office and returned a few seconds later with a piece of paper which he was folding in half. He held it out.

'Thank you. Come, dear,' she said to Fiona, but Alan's hand had closed around the latter's wrist.

'I'm sorry, madam, but this young lady is needed here. She can't be spared for—ah, let me see . . .' he made a great show of consulting his watch, '. . . three-quarters of an hour. Will that be convenient?'

'It certainly will not!' declared Mrs Bottlin-Mabee huffily. 'Obviously I shall have to find another willing helper. I can't wait around for Miss Barclay.' She turned on her heel and stumped off, her entire frame bristling with disapproval. Fiona heaved a sigh of relief and leaned against the wall. Alan reached out to touch her cheek.

'I had to rescue you from her octopus clutches somehow,' he teased. 'God, how my head aches! Fiona, could you spare me a little of your time?' She nodded. 'Good. Then we'll go this way, then we won't meet anyone to tattle on us.'

He reached for her hand and led her along corridors until they arrived at his own cabin. Once there, he gestured to her to shut the door and then flopped wearily into the largest armchair, leaning his head back and closing his eyes.

'Remember how you used to smooth away my headaches?' he murmured, and opened one eye.

'Of course.'

'Five minutes? Please?'

She came over to him and placed her hands firmly on his neck muscles, massaging very gently.

'That horrible woman was right in one thing she said,' Fiona remarked a few seconds later.

'Oh? What was that?'

'You're very tired. Did you sleep at all last night? Sandra said she heard you moving about well into the early hours.'

'No, my love, I didn't sleep.' He lifted his hand and laid it over hers. 'But if you go on like this, I soon shall be,' he finished, with a sleepy smile. He turned his head to drop a light kiss on the back of her hand. She trembled and he glanced up fleetingly before his eyes closed again. 'You know,' he remarked after another long pause, 'I believe Robert was right. It was just a mean twist of fate that that message came when it did. Another few moments ...'

'What do you mean?' she asked, puzzled.

'I've come to the conclusion that you and I are not the most sensible of people, my love. Something will have to be done to correct the stupid mistakes. And ... drat!' The phone intruded loudly, making them both jump.

'Don't answer it!' Fiona urged, aware that he had been about to say something of very great importance.

'I must. I'm the captain, remember? Thanks for the massage, anyway.' He eased himself wearily from the chair and picked up the receiver. 'Yes, Captain speaking. I see. I'll be there at once.' He replaced the receiver and rubbed a tired hand across his forehead. 'Radio room. I was expecting a message. I'll see you later, I hope.'

He came over to her, clasped her shoulders and drew her towards him in a fatherly manner before dropping a light kiss on her forehead. Her fists balled and she steeled herself not to wrap her arms about him.

'There's no time for anything better,' he whispered huskily into her ear. 'When this is over, I want to talk to you. Is that a date?'

'If you wish.'

'Good. I'll keep you to your promise.'

He released her and left the cabin. Fiona's thoughts were not happy. By the time this was over the ship would have docked at home and the voyage have ended. Alan was overtired and his mind busy playing tricks on him. They had nothing more to say to each other.

CHAPTER EIGHT

BY the evening of that first hectic day, the passengers from the Greek ship had been informed that an unscheduled stop would be made at Lisbon for their disembarkation. When the news was made known, Alan was bombarded with questions as to what might happen next, or did his own responsibility end on the dockside?

He assured them that representatives of the holiday company would fly to Lisbon to meet the passengers.

Was everyone obliged to leave at Lisbon? one Scottish passenger wanted to know, because it would be far more convenient for him and his family to remain where they were.

What about compensation? someone else demanded. And was there a choice of rail or air from Lisbon? How about money? There had been no need for Portuguese currency at the start of the abortive cruise.

Was the captain absolutely certain of his facts? He would not just wipe his hands of his extra passengers as soon as they set foot on the dockside thereby leaving them to their own devices?

Copies in all the relevant languages were made of the lengthy radioed reply from the holiday company and pinned to the notice board outside the purser's office for all to read. Fortunately, this seemed to satisfy most of those affected, although many vowed never again to consider another cruise, no matter which shipping line was involved.

Alan had known his presence amongst his new passengers helped to reassure them, but it took a great toll of him following a sleepless and anxious night. His head ached abominably and the mere thought of food nauseated him; even more so after a particularly trying time in the kitchens helping to solve a staffing problem which had arisen.

Wearily he slipped away to his quarters and sank into an armchair, legs sprawled out in front of him. From the night cabin where she had been changing into a fresh skirt and blouse, Fiona heard his movements and paused to listen. When everything was quiet again, she opened the door carefully and tiptoed towards the sleeping man. He did not stir. He looked so exhausted that she was seized with an impulse to stroke back the unruly piece of hair that had flopped across his forehead. He had not even bothered to loosen his tie, she noticed. Deftly she reached for it, moving very, very slowly in order not to waken him. When this was accomplished, she found a footstool, lifted first one leg and then the other and placed them on it. Finally she edged the hand that had flopped over the chair-arm gently on to his lap and crept back to the night cabin as silently as she had arrived.

The disembarkation at Lisbon was carried out with speed and efficiency because Alan could not afford a long stopover in the city. It was not a pleasant day, with grey, overcast skies and a thin drizzle, reminding Fiona poignantly of what possibly lay ahead in England. She and Sandra grinned ruefully at the sight of a long line of ambulances waiting on the dockside.

'I see they're well prepared,' the former remarked.

'Better far too many than too few. And there's little Heidi, of course. She hasn't yet managed to grasp the knack of walking in plaster.'

Even as the words were spoken, Fiona caught sight of the top of Alan's cap as he stepped on to the gangway directly below the two girls, who had stationed themselves at a good vantage point to watch the disembarkation. Alan carried Heidi in his arms and she was chattering away happily in German, while her mother followed behind. They reached the quayside and an ambulance attendant stepped forward to relieve Alan of his burden. Heidi's arms tightened around his neck and he carried her into the vehicle himself.

'He's awfully good with children,' Fiona found herself saying in a gentle tone. Sandra smiled sideways at her.

'Then you know what to do about encouraging it.'

'No, not me. It's too late.'

The thought struck Fiona very forcibly that if she had married Alan three years ago, by now they might have had their own child to hug and kiss.

'I'm going back to pack my things,' she announced hurriedly, and turned from the rail. 'Are you coming?'

'Not for a moment. I want to see Robert in the hospital first, if you don't mind.'

'It'll give me more room to move about!' Fiona grinned. 'I'm glad to be returning to our proper cabin, even if it is only for a few nights.'

Inside the night cabin, Fiona slumped on to the big bed, smoothing the coverlet with her right hand. The emergency was over. Routine as before. If only she had had the courage to suggest that she, too, should disembark at Lisbon and fly home to England! But it had been a stupid moment of fancy, born in a moment of acute misery. Of course she couldn't go off and leave Sandra alone for the remaining few days of the voyage! And there was also the very practical matter of money to pay for the airline ticket, which she did not possess. And, last night, while lying awake beside the sleeping Sandra, she had come to a final decision about Alan's brooch. She had wanted to keep it as a reminder of what might have been, but with the lapse of time she had begun to realise how much pain this must bring her. To see it, day after day, and to know Alan was no longer hers, seemed intolerable in the chill of the night. She must return it to Nancy, and Alan should do the unpleasant job for her. Her conscience had pricked uncomfortably. It was not fair to Nancy. She would not understand. Surely it would be better for Alan to keep the brooch? Or even to throw it into the sea as had been his very first intention?

She would leave it to him to decide. First she had to find a safe place to leave the box where he would not find it before they reached England. It did not matter afterwards how long it took before he discovered the hidden box; at least she ... coward! ... would not be present to witness his reaction.

Alan's steward had emptied the two top drawers for the girls' use and now Fiona gingerly opened the bottom one. It contained sweaters and socks, and probably was not used daily. Even if it were, anything stuffed tightly at the very back would probably lie unnoticed for weeks. This was the ideal hiding-place for her small package.

The day cabin was empty, so she helped herself to a sheet of notepaper and a large elastic band. She returned to the bed and sat down, beginning to write.

'Dear Alan,

By the time you read this I shall have been long gone. I very much want the brooch returned to Nancy, if only you could find a tactful way of doing so without hurting her. I'm sure she will understand why I simply can't keep it. You will, too.

Fiona.'

She folded the paper with care and then wrapped it around the box containing the brooch, keeping it in place with the elastic band. Then she pulled open the bottom drawer, thrust her hand containing the package right to the very back, covered it with woollens and shut the drawer again. That completed, she hurried with her own packing.

It was surprising how swiftly everything seemed to return to normal after the disembarkation, the only difference being the few extra passengers who had elected to continue their journey to England on this vessel.

'You know, Fiona, although I enjoyed helping in the sick bay, it's surprising how tired I now feel,' was Sandra's remark as they dressed for dinner. 'And those Greeks were good fun, even though I'm sure they were passing decidedly risqué remarks about us all the time. As for that Takis——!'

'Enough said about him,' Fiona chuckled in response. 'I was thankful his hands were bandaged, otherwise I'd have been afraid to turn my back on him.'

'Nevertheless, he did very well with his final goodbye kiss.'

Fiona blushed. 'You must put it down to enthusiasm and the Mediterranean temperament. Are you ready? If we don't hurry, we'll be late for dinner.'

A quick glance towards the captain's table showed Fiona Alan's absence and she found herself hoping that he might decide to dine alone in his cabin as a relief from the rush of the past few days. But it was not to be. She had barely started slicing a deliciously cool melon when she caught sight of him. He looked very angry as he strode swiftly into the room. His eyes met and held hers, and her heart stopped. She waited, willing him to pass the table, but he paused at her side, thrust out his arm, uncurled his fingers and showed her the brooch lying in his palm.

'Miss Barclay,' he said in an icy tone, 'you appear to have lost something. I'd be grateful if you would keep it in a safe place. You are familiar, I believe, with the rules regarding jewellery aboard this ship?'

Fiona blushed to the roots of her hair while Mrs Bottlin-Mabee's eyes almost popped out of her head.

'Oh, Captain,' she giggled, 'you really are so droll! That thing's only paste, so it wouldn't matter if Fiona lost it while leaning over the rail to look at the waves!'

The restaurant seemed to swim about Fiona. Alan remained rigid for a second, bowed stiffly to the smiling woman, and then took himself off to his own table. Meanwhile, the American woman on the right of Mrs Bottlin-Mabee reached out a hand to Fiona.

'Could I have a look, please, honey? I know quite a bit about gew-gaws.' Without waiting for Fiona's permission, she scooped the brooch from her hand and peered intently at it. Then she turned a shocked face towards her English companion.

'You're wrong, you know. Quite wrong. This little trinket is very valuable.' She smiled into Fiona's white face and continued soothingly: 'I can see how shocked you are that you nearly lost it. You should do as the captain suggests, take it to the purser's office and have it locked up in his safe unless you're wearing it. Shall I pin it on for you, honey?' Her fingers worked busily before Fiona made any reply. 'There, now it's safe. And the little safety chain, too. Mustn't forget that, must we?'

Mrs Bottlin-Mabee's beady eyes bored into Fiona's forehead, but she was spared any difficult explanations by the sound of someone thumping loudly on a table. Everyone ceased talking and looked towards Alan, who stood at the head of his table, waiting for complete silence.

'Ladies and gentlemen, you will remember that a few nights ago I asked you to join me in a double celebration. Naturally you all took this to mean the engagement of our good doctor and Mrs Stern. I, unfortunately, was called away before I could finish my announcement in its entirety.' There was an excited buzz. He held up his hand and the murmur ceased abruptly.

'By "double", I meant exactly as I said. The celebration was for two happy couples, not one.'

Another buzz of excitement, this time much louder and longer. Colour began to rise in Alan's face.

'Probably I ought not to be the one to do this, but it is the captain's duty. Therefore, may I ask you all to congratulate Miss Fiona Barclay on her engagement?'

Fiona's mouth dropped open and her eyes met Alan's, reading there the love and warmth for which she craved. He beckoned to her.

'Come on, over here, where you belong. A chair will be brought, so you needn't carry it,' he advised as she clung desperately to the back of hers and started to lift it. There was laughter throughout the room. Once again, Alan held up his hand.

'Oh, yes, the very lucky man. I suppose I should tell you...'

The whisper began:

'The Captain!'

'It's *him!*'

Fiona felt tears well up in her eyes as she stumbled towards Alan's table. Eager hands reached out to touch her.

'I hope you'll be very happy, dear.'

'Congratulations!'

'Oh, how lovely for you both!'

She reached Alan's table and he stepped towards her, his arm reaching for her, and drawing her tightly into his side. A great storm of clapping arose.

'Don't you dare deny me now!' he whispered into her ear, but she was too happy and overcome to make any form of protest whatsoever. Reaction would come later, as well as some badly needed explanations! she reminded herself.

Sandra had rushed to her side and was kissing her warmly, then she leaned past to land a kiss on Alan's cheek. He laughed.

'Devils! Sly old devils! You complained enough about me and Robert not saying a word until the announcement—and now this! You're much worse, Fiona, especially as the announcement was supposed to be made on the same evening as ours. Although,' she looked thoughtfully into Fiona's blushing face, 'I wouldn't have thought her behaviour had been exactly loverlike recently.'

'The stress and disappointment of the moment,' Alan slipped in smoothly.

'You could still have told *me*. I'm very good at keeping secrets.'

'I don't expect you to believe me,' Fiona hissed back in a low voice, 'but I didn't even know myself until just now. Alan appears to have a considerable will of his own when it comes to making decisions.'

'My love, your dinner is getting cold,' Robert said at Sandra's side, then beamed at Alan. 'I'm glad you announced it at long last. You were making me quite worried, I can tell you!'

'You knew?' Fiona spluttered.

'Of course. I told him he should have come back later that evening and finished the thing properly, but you know what Alan is ... duty before himself.'

Fiona ate hardly anything of the dinner; her stomach seemed to have tightened into a big ball of happiness, and people bombarded her with questions, many leaving their own tables to come across and congratulate the couple.

'Where's the ring?' an eager woman demanded.

'She'll be wearing it tomorrow.'

'When's the wedding?'

Fiona blushed and Alan answered for her.

'Soon. Very soon.'

'Have you known each other long, or is this another whirlwind shipboard romance, because you both kept the secret extremely well?'

'Fiona and I are friends of very long standing. Our minds were made up some time ago, before the start of the cruise, isn't that so, darling?' His eyes twinkled mischievously at her and she had the grace to blush.

'Yes. Before the start of the cruise.'

The radio officer hurried to Alan's table and handed over a radio message. Without even opening it, Alan remarked to Fiona:

'I can guess what this is. Quite different from the last one I received while making announcements.' He passed the paper to her, unfolded. She read aloud:

'"Every happiness to you both. I demand you visit me soon. Love Nancy."'

'I radioed her a short while ago. I knew you'd want me to.' His gaze caught the soft movement of her hand as it covered the moonstone brooch. 'Moonstones. The stone for tears. No more, eh?' His words were for her alone.

'No more,' she affirmed.

She was blissfully happy, but longing to be alone with Alan to pose the questions in the forefront of her mind.

'I think,' he said at last, 'that you and I will take coffee in my day cabin. Mm?'

'Please!'

They slipped away at the end of the meal, his hand tight about hers. When they reached his quarters, he opened the door and found the steward in the act of placing a coffee tray on the desk. The man beamed at Fiona.

'May I also offer my congratulations, miss?'

'Thank you.'

He vanished discreetly and they were alone. Alan held her at arm's length, then slowly drew her close, his lips meeting hers in a long, long kiss.

'Now, darling, I know you're itching to scold me. I'll pour coffee while you talk.'

'Alan,' she still clung to him, 'why the abrupt change of face?'

'Don't you approve?' he twinkled down at her. 'I know you didn't exactly relish the prospect of being a fallen woman.'

'I dislike being bulldozed. You took me for granted. I didn't have a chance to refuse.'

'That's what I thought. I said to myself, she'll never have the nerve to stand up in front of the whole dining room and say she isn't going to marry me after all. You see, darling,' his face became solemn, 'I just couldn't take the risk of you taking flight yet again. I knew as soon as I saw that brooch stuffed at the back of my drawer that I had to do something quickly.'

'I didn't intend you to find it so soon!' she wailed in protest.

'Nevertheless, I did. I badly need someone to look after me, you see, sweetheart. Most of those socks in the front of the drawer have huge holes in them and are just waiting for your attention.'

'Oh! I never thought of that.'

'Besides, I can't go on running after you much longer because I'm not as young as I used to be. It was a pity that S.O.S. arrived when it did. The crisis made matters so much more difficult for both of us.'

'Yes, I agree. But you were absolutely right not to return to the subject that night. The people aboard the Greek ship were far more important than our private affairs.'

'Robert didn't seem to think so!' Alan chuckled. 'He gave me quite a dressing-down only this afternoon. Was in quite a tizzy because he was under the impression I might possibly lose you if I dilly-dallied much longer. He was right, too, as I learned when I found the brooch. Do you still want coffee, or . . .?'

She arched her neck, reached up to kiss his mouth, the lobe of his ear, his temple. His lips caressed her throat and mouth. With a groan he put her from him but she clutched his hands, holding them to her breasts.

'My love!' he chided. 'You sorely tempt a man.'

'I want to.'

'Hussy. Delicious hussy! You realise you're in danger of losing everything tonight?'

But he put her away from him as he spoke because he knew the force of the great love burning between them. He led her to a chair, sat down in it himself, and swung her up into his lap. Fiona snuggled into him, her hands on his broad chest and her mouth against the vee where his tie had been a moment ago, before her fingers had been at work.

'Why did you change your mind?' she whispered.

He responded with a question of his own.

'Remember asking me to accept your apology?'

'Of course.'

'Now I must apologise to you.'

'For what?'

'For hurting you so much. It wasn't necessary for me to have been so cruel and churlish. You see, a short while ago I wanted to hurt and humiliate you, just as you had humiliated me all those years ago ...'

'Don't! Oh, please, please don't say any more. It isn't necessary. I deserved it, I know I did.'

'I have to explain. I needn't have hurt you so terribly. I know that now and am bitterly ashamed of myself. You see, my pride refused to acknowledge that you were indeed truly sorry for running away before our wedding. I needed to teach you a lesson, or so I thought. When I saw your name on the cruise list, I was furiously angry, believing you to be chasing me. Just because I'd won promotion, you understand. Then I asked myself how could you have known? And I was impatient to see you again. I hoped desperately that it might be you and not another Fiona Barclay. It could have been a cruel trick of fate. Then I saw you and was furious with myself for not trying harder to find you after you ran away. I was stupid to allow your father to dissuade me. I should have persisted in my search and not rested until I'd found you. But I wondered about you since that terrible time.'

'If I hadn't come on this cruise, I doubt whether I should have realised how much I really loved you,' she pointed out gently. 'In the intervening three years I'd grown up.'

'I trod warily, trying to pretend indifference, yet all the time I was deeply conscious of you and the effect you could still command on my emotions. You came to apologise and I couldn't resist the opportunity to mock and degrade you. I thought it was my position you wanted, not me. I wanted then to make you smart, that's why I asked you to become my mistress, though deep within myself I knew you would never countenance such a proposal. I reasoned you might be shocked, as indeed you were. It was then that I really allowed myself to hope. I admired your code of honour. However, at the same time, I realised that if you wanted me just for the glamourised life I now lead, you certainly wouldn't agree to be my mistress. There was my dilemma. When you offered yourself so openly that other night, I knew beyond doubt that you were very much in love with me. The truth was shattering. You can't know how vulnerable you looked, standing here before me, quite defenceless, offering me your body in return for absolutely nothing. Except the love you bore for me.'

He sought her lips hungrily. 'Darling, it was at that moment, the terrible, ghastly moment, that I think I knew the true meaning of love's agony, I wanted to strike you for baring my motives so vividly. And I didn't like myself one little bit. I yearned to catch you in my arms and beg you there and then to marry me after all, but caution stayed my hand. Had I asked you that night, your response would not have come from your heart. You were in a state of great tension, and very afraid. It would have been taking an unfair advantage over you.'

There was a long pause after which she murmured:

'There's one small thing...'

'Yes?'

'You announced the engagement, but I don't seem to recall being asked.'

'But you were, more than three years ago. And I've already put matters in hand for a special licence when we reach home. Or is that too swift for you?'

The love and pride in her eyes gave him his answer.

Harlequin Romance
Beyond the Sweet Waters
ANNE HAMPSON
Harlequin Romance
The Arrogant Duke
ANNE MATHER
Cap Flamingo
VIOLET WINSPEAR
Teachers Must Learn
NERINA HILLIARD
4 FREE
Harlequin Romances